I0682960

A Horse for My Kingdom

Tales from the Quaquaverse, Volume 1

A.P. John

Published by Quaquaverse Press, 2024.

A HORSE FOR MY KINGDOM

First edition. January 1, 2024.

Copyright © 2024 A.P. John.

ISBN: 979-8986620435

Written by A.P. John.

A Word to the Wise

FROM A.P. JOHN

Let the Reader Beware

What follows is not necessarily a good story well told. But it is a story. That much I guarantee.

I wrote this story because it gave me a laugh and a tingle in my trousers. I hope it offers you the same pleasures. The sense of humor is my own, perhaps only my own, and it is rife with sex, violence, toilet humor, puns, parody, farce, and slapstick. The violence and jokes primarily fill the spaces between the sexy parts.

Most importantly, please understand this is an *adult fantasy* story, with emphasis on *fantasy*. If you seek laughter and titillation, you're at the right window. If you are looking for anything else, like *A Story of Great Moral Import* or, gods save us, *A Good Example for the Children*, you will find what you seek over there, in that rapidly growing library section overseen by the humorless and perpetually outraged ochlocrats in the Ministry for Ruining Everybody's Fun.

In short: *Ye buys yer ticket, an' ye takes yer chances.* ***Caveat Lector.***

Chapter 1 - Easier to Fight a Tree Cat

Oben stood knee-deep in the crisp, icy water of the rushing stream, wearing nothing but the large, sheathed knife on his leather belt.

People usually traveled in pairs this far from his village. Alone, a knife and a wary eye were all he had. Outside the gates of Barada lurked tree cats and wild dogs, huge rock snakes and the small but ferocious weasels of extreme orneriness.

But the most dangerous creature walked on two legs, wore clothes, carried weapons, and was always to be feared.

And these were just the mortal dangers.

Oben feared these and many other things. Most things, in fact, scared the water out of Oben.

He was tall and strong, muscled from a young lifetime spent as apprentice blacksmith to his father. Outdoor work and the blast of the forge had tanned his skin, and long, thick auburn hair framed his handsome, chiseled face. His body could endure hard work and hardship, and his long, muscular legs could carry him over many miles before tiring.

His only weakness lay in his heart. Somehow, an imp of fear had made its home there.

The hissing growl of a tree cat wheeled him around, knife in hand, dribbling pee into the crystal, flowing water of the stream.

"Eah!" he squealed, stabbing the air with his knife, "Eah, agh! Get back, you-"

He stopped shrieking and peeing when he saw Nios, standing on the bank and laughing at him, her teeth gleaming white under her glistening green eyes.

"You," he said, sheathing his knife and blushing, "you and your tree cat imitation. Doesn't that ever get old?"

"When you stop falling for it," she said, still laughing, "then it will get old."

"You have a very big mean streak."

"And you," Nios said, her smile still bright, "I swear to Tyl and all his horny little demons, have a very small cock."

He turned away from her. "The water is cold."

"Oh, is that your excuse?" Nios leaned her back against a tree and set a foot on it, showing a shapely calf below the hem of her simple blue skirt. "Why don't you come get it warm, and we'll see what happens?"

"Trust me," Oben said, lowering his tone, "you don't want to see it angry."

"I've seen it angry. Don't you remember?"

"Yes, but that was before. I made a promise to your father."

"I didn't promise anything," she said, waving her leg back and forth. "You could just lie back and let me do all the work."

"There's that mean streak again."

Oben glanced at the sky. Father Sun was about to set, turning the eastern clouds yellow and orange. Tiny Daughter Sun followed, still climbing Mount Tamberlain and casting the white light of her wedding veil in the western sky behind her.

When The Father went home behind Mount Fire, ending his workday to spend the evening with his wife, Moa, Mother-of-All, he'd leave his beloved daughter behind to stand beside Warrior Moon. The celestial couple would then walk the path to the altar to be married among the stars, as they had done every evening since long before the world was born.

"It's getting late," Oben said.

He waded toward where his clothes hung on a tree branch. "Have you come out here just to tease me, or did you have some purpose?"

"Both," Nios said, moving slowly along the bank, "I love to tease you, and your father wants you."

"I told him where I was going. I worked hard today, smithing shoes for all the constable's horses. I needed a bath."

"Yes, but he asked me to tell you to hurry." She made the last few steps and snatched his tunic and pants from the branch. "He has a task for you."

Oben stopped when he reached the bank, shaking the water off his body in a spray of bright droplets. "A task, huh? Some shit-shoveling errand, no doubt, which will make me late for supper, and he'll get all the chicken feet soup."

Nios held his clothes to her breast. "Actually, it sounds very important."

"Hmm. Why did he send you and not my stupid little brother, Oily?"

"Well, I was at your house, with my father, and-"

"What's your father got to do with this?"

"Um," Nios faltered a moment as she picked up his boots, then said, "Well, he's the one who suggested you for the task."

Oben eyed the tall, raven-haired girl he'd known all his life. He took a turn smiling. "This is just another of your cruel jokes, isn't it?"

"No, honestly. Your father and mine are waiting for you. They said to hurry."

He held out his hand. "Then give me my clothes so I can go."

She took a step back, still clutching his things, and her wily smile returned. "Instead of that," she said, "how about I take my dress off and we'll see if that angers your cold, little thing?"

"You said I was to hurry."

"It won't take long. It didn't before."

He smirked at her, "You're engaged again."

"Yes," she sighed, "but this one won't last either. Father keeps engaging me to these shit-brains, and I keep chasing them off. This one is the son of a wealthy fertilizer merchant, so quite literally a shit-brain. He won't last another week."

"And anyway," she said, then sing-songed, "I'm not married *yet*."

She threw Oben that smile again and added a wag of her expressive black eyebrows for effect.

Oben dropped his chin to break away from those searching eyes and tamp down his yearning.

He thought back to when they were babes, born under the same moon, only a few days apart, how their mothers would bathe them together, then set them down on soft fur rugs to play. It started then, he remembered, his deep desire to be near her, to touch her.

Or maybe it started much earlier.

That smile, he thought, *I've seen it on her since before she had teeth. Always bright and always somewhat mean, a coy but cruel twist to her mouth as if she knew something, or everything, and was keeping it all to herself like a miser with gold.*

"Nios," he said, "When your father first promised you in marriage to, uh, who was the first?"

"Trantek. That drunken wine wholesaler from Aflax"

"Yes, Trantek. I begged your father to choose me, but he chose Trantek because he was rich."

"He wants the best for me."

"Yes, and so do I. So I promised him, and myself, never to touch you again."

"And you've kept your word," she said, pouting, "you rotten bastard. I'd hate you for it if I didn't love you so desperately."

"And when you chased Trantek off by wallowing in horse dung and screeching like a wood devil-"

Her bright smile returned, "Pretty good act, wasn't it?"

"Yes. You should join a theatre troupe. You're missing your calling."

"My calling," she said, dropping her eyelids and lifting the hem of her skirt to reveal her shapely thigh, "is to get your cock hard, then make you erupt like Mount Fire, so you cry my name in your sleep and never leave my side."

Again, Oben looked away from her tantalizing beauty and fought down the desire she sparked.

Without the slightest touch, standing a dozen feet away, the allure of her called to him in scent, sight, and vibration, the wordless and songless siren call of a woman at home in her body, passing that spirit to a man with nothing more than a glance.

"Not without your father's consent," he struggled to say. "Gustall is the Chief Magistrate of Barada and your father. I've asked him again every time you pull some stunt and make your betrothed run for the hills. If you chase this new one off, I'll ask again. But until he agrees, I must keep my vow."

"Bastard," she said, still smiling and swishing her skirt to show her legs. "Wouldn't you like just a quick rub-out? I would. Your fingers have magic that makes me melt and shiver, and you always enjoyed my two-hander, didn't you?"

Oben faltered, the blood warming in his veins, and stammered, "Enjoyment is... is not the point, because-"

"You're right," she said, "Love is the point. I love you, you love me, and what we do together shatters worlds and creates new ones. We've never put our bodies together, like The Father and Moa, to create a new life, a child. But that is what I want, what Ludd wants, what I need."

"Nios, please-"

"Yes, *please*," she panted, her skirt now high and showing herself brazenly, "if you won't put yourself into me, at least touch me."

"Oh, Nios."

She gently laid a finger near her cleft and winked, "How about this? You rub me till I burst, and I'll do that thing with my mouth you like. Remember? That time behind the forge, with the heat of the fire making us sweat?"

Oben remembered. His body was drying, and warming, and the reveries kicked sparks in his belly that burst into tiny flames past his navel. He felt his flesh rise.

Her eyes caught sight of the change and widened, "I see we're on to something."

She reached for the laces of her bodice, "I'll just get out of this-"

"No!" he shouted, and she stopped.

"You're engaged and we're not married and that's that!"

Nios rolled her eyes and cursed, "By Ludd, you've sure been fooled by those priests, haven't you?"

He moved toward her, his hand out, "Give me my clothes."

She recovered her smile and stepped backward. "I'll make you a deal. If you can catch me before we reach the village gate-"

He tried to add menace to his voice, but his now firming manhood gave away his weakness, "I said," he growled, "give me my-"

And she was off, her black tresses flying, laughter rippling through the trees, her lean legs carrying her away so fast she disappeared beyond a stand of bushes before he could blink.

He knew she would not stop. If he didn't catch her, she would run all the way to his house, hide his clothes, and pretend to their fathers she'd never found him. He would have to sneak into the village and all the way home, past the gate guards and the people preparing for their evening meal, stark naked.

If he caught her, well, it could be worse.

His cock, from all appearances, preferred the worse outcome.

Resigned to the worst, Oben pressed it against his belly with his hand to keep it from flopping and sprinted after his best and most frustrating friend.

Chapter 2 - Danger, Magic, and Traveling Salesmen

Father Sun disappeared behind Mount Fire, leaving Daughter Sun and Warrior Moon to begin their nightly courtship. As they made their way toward the altar high in the heavens, Oben's mother was happily hosting the Chief Magistrate of Barada in her humble home.

"More chicken feet soup, Your Honor?"

The magistrate, rotund and resplendent in his off-the-rack doublet of blue silk and horsehair, said, "Oh dear me, thank you, but no more, dear woman. You've stuffed me to the jowls already."

"Save room for dessert, Gustall," Oben's father said, "Tulee bakes the most delicious Figgy Mouse pie."

"Oh, Crent," Tulee said, blushing, "you do go on, don't you?"

"Oi wanna mouse poi" cried second-son Ollie, banging his feet against the table legs and whining.

"Shut up and finish your soup," Crent growled, "then get out there and clean up the shop before bed."

Ollie sniveled, "Why should Oi do et? Oben do!" The spotty-faced pre-teen wiped his runny nose with his hand and dragged the slime through his wispy yellow hair.

"Your brother worked hard today," Tulee said, "And he needs to prepare for a big job tomorrow, so finish your soup, dear, and hurry."

Ollie pointed his spoon at the magistrate, splashing his doublet with broth and tiny shreds of chicken feet, "He ated all da feet! Bad man!"

Gustall daubed at his coat with a kerchief and scowled at the skinny, pubescent boy.

Crent said, "Get out there and clean up now or I'll sell you to the Thief Gnomes!"

"Whaaaah!" Ollie wailed, making the three adults grimace and cover their ears, "Oi wanna figgy mouse!"

"Go!"

The boy screeched all the way out of the house and to the blacksmith shop beyond. They heard the angry clanging of iron tools and thuds of wood against wood.

"You shouldn't threaten the boy with the Thief Gnomes," Tulle chided her husband.

"My father threatened to sell me to the Gnomes, and it didn't do me any harm."

"Yes, but he actually did sell your sister."

"She deserved it. And it showed he was serious. Kept the rest of us in line."

Tulee turned and gave the magistrate an embarrassed smile, "We're sorry to bother you with our family problems, Your Honor."

Gustall waved her off with a slight grin and continued dabbing at the spots.

Crent said, "More ale, Your Honor?"

"Yes, thank you."

"Coming right up." He went to the pantry room for another bottle.

Tulee wrung her hands in a kitchen cloth, "I do wish you'd tell us what you have in store for Oben," she said, "The suspense is killing me."

"Apologies, dear woman, but I wish to tell Oben first. I hope my daughter finds him and brings him soon. The hour is growing late."

Crent returned with two bottles of ale and filled his guest's tankard, "Oh, come on, Gusty," he said, "we're friends since we were pups. Give us a hint, won't you?"

The man downed half his ale and, with a satisfied grin, said, "Oh, very well. Just this. Your firstborn has grown to become an extraordinary blacksmith, as you know."

Crent smiled with feigned humility, "Well..."

"If you hadn't whelped that little creature out there drooling down his shirt, I'd have thought your sperm was blessed by Ludd himself."

Crent's grin melted into a scornful frown at his wife.

Tulee returned the look and threw her husband a two-fingered salute.

"And even more to my purpose," Gustall said, "he's a brilliant horseman. It's astounding how even the most wild-eyed stallion is made like a faithful lapdog at his word and a touch of the muzzle."

"Ah, yes," Tulee said, her face beaming with pride. She frowned again at Crent. "He gets that from my side."

The magistrate looked askance at the proud mother. "Yes, well, be that as it may, it is these skills on which I hope to rest my trust. I require his talent to carry out a vital and dangerous mission."

"Dangerous?" Tulee gasped. "But that sounds dangerous." She heel-slapped her forehead three times to ward off evil.

"But vital," the magistrate countered, "to Barada, and to us. If we succeed, our little hamlet will gain favor with the king and garner his largess. You could receive commissions for blacksmithing services to the court, perhaps to King Otto himself! He might promote me to Super-Chief Magistrate. Barada could receive franchising rights to sell royal trinkets!"

"Ooh," Tulee said, "I would love one of those Queen Syllabub bobble heads."

"You, Crent, could hire apprentice smiths and retire in luxury."

Oben's father scowled, "But I don't want to retire. Blacksmithing is my life."

The magistrate gave Crent a clap on the shoulder. "And that, my oldest friend, is exactly why I am wearing silk and horsehair, and you are wearing lowly homespun."

"Hey," Tulee said, "I spanned that homespun." She glanced at the ceiling, her hand to her chin. "Spinned? Spunned?"

At the sound of footfalls and labored breathing, all turned to watch the door, left open when Ollie ran out to the blacksmith shop.

Oben appeared in the doorway first, then Nios, both breathless and disheveled.

"Oh my Ludd," Tulee said, going to her son, "what happened to you?"

She began picking leaves and twigs from his hair and clothes.

Nios clutched Oben's arm and said, "He fought a tree cat."

Crent rose from the table. "A tree cat?" He eyed Nios, as decorated with debris from the forest floor as was Oben. "Then what happened to you?"

"I, um. I helped."

"Helped?"

"We wrestled it together."

Gustall stood. "A tree cat? Nobody wrestles with a tree cat and lives."

"Well," Nios said, elbowing Oben in the ribs and smiling, "it was a pussy of some sort."

Oben cleared his throat and said, "Really, there was no danger."

"Not to me, more's the pity," Nios whispered.

Tulee stepped back and pointed at Oben's crotch, "What is that stain, son?"

Oben stammered, "I, uh, fell into a wet patch."

Nios again whispered, "Almost."

Crent said, "Oh, you poor dear," and went to Nios, "Here, let me help you."

Oben's father began brushing debris from her dress, his hands lingering over her breasts and down her midriff to her wide hips.

She smiled as one hand arrived at her firm, rounded haunch. Still smiling, she stepped closer and lifted her pale, rose-cheeked face close to his, her lips parted slightly. As Crent fell under her spell, she delivered a sharp jab under his breastbone, making him grunt and stagger back, coughing.

Tulee saw all this and smiled.

Gustall said, "What's the matter, old man?" and helped his friend sit at the table.

"Nothing," Crent croaked, "Al.. Allergies."

"Nios!" Ollie suddenly ran in and clutched the beautiful girl at her waist, burying his greasy face into her breast and humping her thigh like a crazed beagle.

"Oily! Stop that!" Oben shouted.

Tulee shook a finger, "Don't call your little brother that."

Nios smiled again, "Oh, don't worry about him. He'll be fine."

As she spoke, she wrapped one arm around his greasy head and firmly pressed the edge of her other hand against the side of the boy's neck.

Oben stammered, "But... but..."

Everyone watched as Ollie's pelvic undulations slowed, his eyes drooped, his arms lost their grip, and his knees buckled.

Nios released her hold, and Ollie slumped to the floor.

"Poor child is tired," she said, "You work him too hard."

Tulee gazed at her unconscious son, then at Nios. "Teach me to do that, will you?"

"Ahem," grumbled the magistrate, "perhaps later. Time is fleeting, and I must confer with your firstborn about my plan."

"Of course, your honor," Tulee said, taking a blanket from a nearby chair and covering Ollie where he lay.

Gustall approached and wrapped his arm around Oben's shoulder, "Young man, I have a proposition for you that, should you accept it and succeed, will make you wealthy and famous, bring fortune to your family and honor to your village."

"Yes?" Oben said, his voice thinned by his fluttering heart.

"Indeed. Your skill as a blacksmith and a natural handler of horseflesh makes you the perfect man for the job."

"Me?" he croaked.

"You."

Oben glanced at Nios, whose radiant smile and loving eyes strengthened his spleen, "What would you have me do?"

"The great magician Zag, Grand Vizier to King Otto, has entrusted to me the great task of delivering a gift to the king himself."

"What sort of gift?"

"A magic horse."

"Magic?"

Tulee echoed, "Magic?"

Crent, likewise, "Magic?"

Gustall shrugged, "So the man says. But no matter. I need your skill, dear Oben, to take this horse, possessed of sorcery and bewitchment or simply full of hay, over the Forked Road to the king's castle at Tamberlain, and deliver him, personally, to King Otto."

"The Forked Road?" Crent said.

"The Forked Road?" Tulee repeated.

Oben said, "The-"

"Yes, damn it to Tyl!" Gustall shouted, "The Forked Road!"

Oben sputtered, "But... but the Forked Road passes through the... the..."

"By Ludd," Nios sighed, "I'll say it. The Forked Road passes through the dreaded Forest of Unholy Creatures Killing All Loitering Luddians."

"Yes," said the magistrate, "You'll have to pass through Fuckall to get there."

Oben's face drained of blood, "That's where the Thief Gnomes live."

"And worse than that, my son," Crent said, "There are wizards, and ghosts..."

"Banshees," Tulee whispered, and heel-slapped her forehead.

"Wood Devils," Gustall whispered and stuck his fingers up his nose to avoid breathing the evil words he just uttered.

"Worst of all," Nios said, "Traveling Salesmen."

The three parents gasped.

Oben fainted.

Chapter 3 - Just Another Night at the Dog and Duck Inn

Later that night, Daughter Sun and Warrior Moon stood at the high altar exchanging their vows.

Beneath, the people of Barada reveled in celebration, imbibing and gambling under the high-gabled roof of the Dog and Duck Inn. Lusty women plied their trade among the rough and rowdy patrons, delivering tankards of ale, quick kisses, and promises of glandular relief to one increasingly drunk male after another. Dice clattered and coins clanked while laughter and wicked oaths escaped the open windows and rose through the branches of the majestic pines to mix with the warm night breezes of high summer.

Flap the Archer and Dongle the Oaf sat at a corner table away from the loudest of the clamor, waiting for their childhood friend Oben to arrive. The misbegotten little brother Oben called Oily had told them, through giddy and phlegmatic gibberish, that his brother was to embark on the high adventure he'd always craved and wished that his friends would accompany him.

The short, thin bowman and the massive, human bovine waited, Flap nursing a small tin cup of wine while Dongle drained his fourth tankard of ale, belched loud enough to rattle the rafters, and reached for his fifth.

"Tyl take the hindmost," Flap moaned, holding his nose, "must you expel so great a quantity of gaseous stench with every gulp?"

"Huhhehhuh, Dongle thirsty", rumbled the massive man-child, and quaffed the fifth ale.

Gleda the innkeeper, endowed with three women's worth of breast and buttock, passed by the table, four tankards clutched in each of her meaty hands.

Flap raised his cup and said, "Oh, dear madame of the house?"

Gleda stopped and turned, portions of her bulk making the shift later than others.

"Wot is et, ya walkin' twig?"

"At your earliest convenience, of course, would you be so kind as to bring me another cup of this fine Tamberlain Red, and another half-dozen or so frothy buckets for my friend?"

"I've got these ta drop first, ya wee pillock. I'll get ta ya when I can, aye?"

"Indubitably."

"An' ya'll pay in coin this time, nay more on th' cuff fer ya."

"Of course, madame, my fortune is about to arrive."

"An' by-the-by, I'm nay madame, little prick. Just 'cause the servin' girls 'ere will on 'casion get a bit flirty wif' da clientele, an' each has a wee bunk upstairs where dey can, o' dere own free will, take a gent'man caller for a bit o' simple fun, and if dey so wish, require of such a gent'man da fare o' five coins fer a bit o' bed romp, seven if he asks special favors, dat don't make me a procurer!"

Flap smiled, "Well, my pretty and plentiful patroness, I'll have you know that I have availed myself of that same simple fun with most of your girls, and so attentive am I to their tasty, vibrating little buttons of love that I am regularly afforded a twenty percent discount."

Gleda's bulbous nose raised and sniffed, "Dat's not my lookout. Discounts cut from dere share, not mine."

The impressive vessel known as Gleda sailed off.

"A fine woman," Flap mused and drained the last of his Red.

"Dongle like Gleda bum," said the smiling oaf, "Go boom-bam real good one time. She not happy when Dongle go spurt."

"Nobody's happy when Dongle go spurt," Flap laughed. "Entire communities have been washed away."

Oben stepped through the massive log door of the inn and made his way to the table where his friends waited.

Flap raised his empty cup. "Greetings, oh mighty captain. Sit and I will order wine and meat for you, on my tab, of course."

As Oben sat, Dongle's massive face split into a half-toothed grin.

"Oben good!" he declared and clapped the blacksmith on the back, slamming his forehead to the table.

Oben sat up, dazed and rubbing his brow as the wily archer cut his purse from his belt and waved down a pretty, redheaded tavern maid.

He gave her the purse and whispered, "Do me the favor of giving this to Gleda for my tab, and keep three for yourself, my luscious little strawberry."

She smiled, pecked the archer's cheek, and ran off.

"Well then," Flap said, "keep us in suspense no longer, glorious leader. Your golum told us we were to accompany you on a grand adventure. Is it really true? After all these years?"

"Yes, it's true," Oben said. "I've been given a task of vital importance and great danger."

Flap said, "Oh? You say that with such lack of enthusiasm, I might think you're joking or still recovering from Dongle's greeting. Yours is the face of a man waiting on the gallows steps, third in line to be hanged."

"Didn't you hear me say great danger?"

"Yes, but danger is the wife of adventure, and when they copulate, beautiful children are conceived."

"Huhhehhuh. Boom-bam!"

"In a word."

"Magistrate Gustall asked me to deliver a gift to King Otto."

"That's your marvelous adventure? Errand boy to a third-rate civil servant?"

"The gift is a horse."

"So? You handle equines as I handle bow and blade, with masterly skill and to great effect."

Oben scowled, "What's the shortest road to Tamberlain?"

Flap glanced up. "Let's see, there's... Oh, Ludd. Fuckall!"

"Exactly."

"The Forked Road," Flap whispered and slapped his forehead three times.

Dongle's eyes widened like full moons. "Nuhhhh! Hunnnuhhhnuhhh!" the oversized baby grunted, pounding the table with his sledgehammer fists.

The two men struggled to calm Dongle, grabbing at his tree-trunk arms, cooing lullabies, and begging his quiet.

But the man-bear's voice only lifted in volume and pitch. "Nuhh nuaaay nuoooo! Fuuucked Rooooad! Noouuhhh!" His pounding began splintering the table's slats and drowning out the clamor of the inn.

Finally, Flap drew the heavy club of petrified wood from the giant's belt and, two-handed, clouted Dongle's crown like a clapper to a huge church bell.

This silenced the oaf, and the room, every man in witness, ready to escape, should Dongle confound all attempts at control.

The smile on the now-quiet man's face drew sighs of relief. He wobbled slightly in his chair, grinning, then declared, "Flap good!" and with an affectionate back slap, caromed the archer's pate against the tabletop.

The patrons returned to their carousing; the laughter more raucous than before in celebration of having cheated Death.

The appearance of Nios at the threshold added the steam of lust to the already overheated atmosphere of the tavern.

Men whistled like songbirds and hooted like owls, calling out her name and making promises of sexual acrobatics few, if any, could fulfill. Women scowled at her and cursed, some throwing their hands up in surrender and arranging trysts with their sisters in despair of stealing one male glance away from the raven-haired goddess.

She made her way through the tables slowly, hips swaying as to move the tides, leaving in her wake the scentless scent of womanhood, ageless as the drifting continents, promising solace and sorrow, fecundity and futility.

As if deaf and blind to the surrounding clamor, she strode toward and stared into the eyes of the only man in existence. Reaching him, she cupped his chin with her soft hand and laid the lightest kiss on his lips.

The crowd roared with a mixture of delight and despondency.

"Hello Oben," she purred.

Oben's mouth moved but, lacking breath, made no sound.

Flap rose and doffed his feathered cap, bowed and said, "Accept of me my deepest gratitude for the simple fact that you live, dear Nios."

She dipped her chin and her eyes in sultry thanks.

"Huhhehhuh" grunted Dongle, his smile and bright eyes some odd mixture of childish delight and lecherous leer, "Nios! Boom-bam!"

She stepped past Oben and greeted the massive man, drawing a delicate finger down his spine from the nape of his neck past his shoulder blades.

"Dear, sweet Dongle," she cooed.

"Huhhehhuh Huhhehhuh Huhhehhuh!" he gurgled and grunted.

Flap watched with wary eyes. "Dongle, lad, take care now."

Her hand now pressed against his spine just above his belt, Nios bent toward him, the cleft of her bosom flowing as if to beckon a kiss, her faint bouquet scrambling the little sense he possessed.

Nios whispered in his ear, "Dear. Sweet. Dooongle."

The oaf's face now collapsed as if turning in on itself, eyes squeezed shut, massive jaw clenched. A low moan arose from deep in the cavern of his chest, as if a minotaur trapped in a labyrinth bellowed in captive agony.

Oben and Flap gasped, stood, and stepped back.

"No boy!" Flap shouted, "Don't do it!"

The crowd held its breath. Some of the strongest men bolted for the door.

A great rhythmic pounding began, lifting the table in waves, a boom, boom, boom, like a god come down from the heavens to stroll over the mountains to the sea.

Flap and Oben put more distance between themselves and the impending eruption, while Nios remained at his side, her breath warming his cheek.

The pounding increased in speed and seismic depth.

From behind the bar, Gleda screamed, "Nay! Not again!"

Judging the moment, Nios gently nibbled the top of the man's ear.

Dongle's eyes and mouth suddenly gaped. His breath stopped. The thundering under the table ceased.

"Boom!" shouted the oaf, then lost the power of speech.

Shattering the silence, the sound of a dozen milkmaids dumping their pails on the floor, followed by a heaving sigh from the relieved hulk.

From the assembled Baradans, a great susurration of exhales and gasps.

There followed a massive funk reaching every nostril, some indiscernible admixture of afterbirth and ancient oceans.

Oben stared in wonder at Nios, now standing with hands on hips and smiling at him with haughty triumph.

"What can I say?" she shrugged. "It's a gift."

"You'll clean dat up, ya will," shouted innkeeper Gleda. "It'll eat out the joins 'tween da floorboards!"

Flap said, "I'll get some buckets."

Chapter 4 - No More for Me, Thanks, I'm Questing

A s Oben and Nios were wringing the last of the drenched rags into the nearly full pails, Dongle lay sprawled over half the table, snoring in blissful, dreamless sleep.

Flap carried away the last two buckets filled with an empire's worth of potential taxpaying citizens. The tavern was now host to only a handful of temperate patrons. Some had left for home, while most had absconded upstairs.

Flap returned to his friends carrying hot, wet towels, three tin cups and a full bottle of Gleda's best red. The dark, curiously shaped bottle came not from their home capital of Tamberlain, but from the castle of their sovereign's rival, King Hod of Aflax.

Washing themselves, Oben mentioned the expensive, contraband wine.

"It seems" Flap said as he poured, "that the performance of prodigious priapism from the super-human inseminator here, sparked and inflamed by our lovely muse, has aroused a considerable number of customers to heights of sexual tension. As we speak, they are pouring coin into the purses of the ladies upstairs while pouring great rivers of man-seed into their quivering quims."

Nios smiled. "I believe it's called 'priming the pump.'"

Flap said, "Indubitably. Our sweet and gentle hostess sends this bottle with her thanks and asks if we might wish to book our little pantomime for a season's run. Say, three nights a week and twice on Sundays?"

Oben said, "That's ridiculous."

"I play a passable three-string tonka," Flap said, "and I know many ribald songs."

"No."

Nios asked, "What would it pay?"

"Dear Gleda opened the bidding at ten percent, but I know we could get her to twenty."

Oben looked at Nios, her face inscrutable. "You can't seriously think-"

"Maybe for thirty" she said, "We'll have expenses."

Flap smiled, "I'll see what I can do." He raised his cup. "Meanwhile, here's to the theatre."

The three companions quaffed a salute.

Flap sighed appreciably and said, "Well, stout captain? What's the story of this grand adventure that will likely end with our souls damned to the dark place, our bodies defiled, and our bones hung from trees?"

"Nothing" Oben said, keeping his eyes in his cup, "I'm going to tell the magistrate I won't do it."

Flap and Nios both set down their drinks and said, "What?"

"He can find another fool."

Nios said, "But you already promised my father you would start out tomorrow morning."

"It wasn't a promise. I said I'd consider it."

Her dark brows furrowed. "You did not. Before he and I left your house you clearly said, 'Yes, Your Honor, I will do it."

"I'm changing my mind."

"I won't let you."

Oben frowned at the beautiful woman. "What do you mean, won't let me? I can change my mind if I want."

"No" Nios said quietly, her eyes glistening into Oben's, "you can't."

Flap said, "Perhaps some compromise is in order. It's true the Forked Road is the fastest route to Tamberlain, as long as one isn't killed, that is. But why not take the mountain road?"

Nios still held Oben's eyes prisoner. He broke away and stared into the blood-red wine.

"Because the horse must be in Tamberlain in time for the king's joust, three days hence. The mountain road would take a week."

"Ah, I see."

"The horse is a gift to the king from Zag, the Grand Vizier."

All three slapped their foreheads.

"He claims it's a magic steed that, ridden by Otto, will guarantee our king's victory in his joust against Hod."

Flap nodded. "Something very much to be desired, as Hod is a cruel and stupid man-child, unfit to rule a mud puddle. But I'm not fond of this new way of solving disputes, kings jousting, winner take all. I prefer a good old-fashioned battle, thousand men a side, armor clashing, great lakes of blood, etcetera. There's too much at stake to rely on the prowess of one man."

"I like the new way" Nios said. "Most feuds between kings are nothing more than cock-measuring contests, and don't need the lives and limbs of a thousand men to resolve. I say strip the two naked, give each a club and mark a circle in the dirt. Last one standing is king of all, and we can go on with our lives in peace."

Flap raised his cup. "You make a compelling argument."

Oben said, "It must be a joke of some kind, though. A magic horse?"

"You know full well that magic is real, my friend" Flap said. "You just witnessed it in the purest form, the bewitchment this sorceress cast over our mindless but not glandless friend here."

"That wasn't magic" Nios said, her smile bright and haughty, "that was technique."

"Call it what you will, it amounts to the same thing."

Oben was quiet a moment, staring at the table, then said, "Well, magic or not, I'm not risking my life, and my friends' lives on a fool's errand."

Flap sighed, "Look, old boy, you've been wishing for this moment your entire life. You could barely walk before you were casting your eye to the far side of the mountains. As boys we played at knights and dragons, but you told me in blood oath that you would fight actual dragons one day."

"This winter past" Nios added, "you were regaling us with a plan to sail the seas in search of treasure and high adventure."

"And I will" Oben said, "on my own terms and time. But this is just foolishness. Travelers on the Forked Road disappear all the time, and the ones who are found, or what's left of them, tell of an evil there more deadly than any tree cat."

Nios sighed, "Oh, Oben."

"There will be other chances. My day of adventure will come."

"This maybe it, chum" Flap said. "There may never come another. Fortune favors the brave, and the brave do not quibble over whether this or that challenge is to be taken. It could be your first, last and only chance."

"I'm brave" Oben said, his face declaring the opposite, "I'm just wise as well. They say, 'discretion is the better part of valor.'"

"Cowards say that" Nios said, staring into her wine.

"Nios, please."

"No, I do not please" she said, her eyes now burning into Oben's. "You know I love you. I always have and I always will. I want to marry you. But I'll not wed a coward."

Oben stared, stunned. "But I'm not, not-"

"At the risk of pedantry" Flap said, "Memento Mori. Remember Thou Wilt Die. Seize the Day. Gather ye rosebuds while ye may. Have It Your Way. Just Do It."

Oben looked from Flap to Nios, then downed the last of his wine and closed his eyes, fighting back tears.

Struggling herself, Nios said, "My beloved, if you don't face your fears and take this challenge, I will marry the shit-brain my father has chosen for me. And I'll never speak to you again."

Oben raised his eyes to hers, jaw clenched, and brow furrowed, his breath coming in short gulps.

A great bellow of "Nios!" from the door turned every head.

Magistrate Gustall stomped through the room to the trio's table. "Girl, what are you doing here?"

"I'm drinking with my friends, father. And I'm no girl."

"You're more girl than woman, that's certain."

"If you'd seen her earlier, Your Honor" Flap said, "you would not say that."

"Come home, Nios, you must prepare for the wedding."

Oben stood, knocking over his empty cup. "Wedding?"

"Didn't she tell you?" Gustall said, "I'll see you off tomorrow morning, with the king's gift. Then come the noon bell my daughter marries Scut of Weewax, son to Craps of Weewax."

"Craps?" Flap said, smiling. "The dung dealer?"

"Purveyor of fine, restorative mulch" Gustall corrected.

"A shit-brain!" Oben shouted, punching the table with his knuckles.

Gustall said, "I beg your pardon?"

Oben and Nios locked eyes, both angry and silent.

A moment arrived, then passed, as moments are wont to do.

"Come, Nios" her father said, holding out his arm for her.

Nios allowed another moment to pass, watching, waiting, then dropped her gaze.

She whispered, "Remember what I said."

"Daughter?"

She rose and took his arm. "Yes, father."

Without glancing back, Nios followed her father from the Dog and Duck.

Oben stood unmoving, staring at the door.

Gleda passed by, carrying tankards.

"I has an idea, I has" she said, grinning brightly. "If I puts a horse trough under th' table afore ye arrives, the cleanin' up after'll be easier, aye?"

Flap said, "Yes, brilliant thought, my pretty pachyderm. That is..."

He looked to Oben, "...that is, if we agree to a return engagement. What say ye, captain, director, sir?"

The blacksmith rapped the table with his knuckles.

"Come to my house at dawn" he said.

Dongle stirred, grumbled, and farted. "Ohhh, Dongle bad" he groaned.

"And bring him with you."

"Aye, captain."

Oben strode across the tavern and out the door.

Gleda watched, then said to Flap, "Well? Ten percent, then?"

Flap stood and said with a bow, "Apologies, dear madame, but it seems our troupe of titillating troubadours has a prior engagement."

Chapter 5 - A Horse with a Difference, and What a Difference

T he celestial couple escaped for their honeymoon as Father Sun rose over the western peak of Mount Tamberlain to begin another day's loving labor as The Great Provider.

Oben, Flap and Dongle waited by the village well, silent, squinting into the sunrise that lit their path. Flap wore his best tunic and tights, his bow, quiver of arrows, and three-stringed tonka over his shoulders. A short sword hung sheathed at the ready, and a small bag of tools and provisions hung at his side.

Dongle carried little beyond his heavy club. The man could take sustenance on a long trek simply by eating whatever was at hand: leaves and bark, insects, small animals or their leavings, and was entirely impervious to the elements. In a pinch, he could get down on all fours and serve as an emergency shelter for his companions.

Oben stood proudly, shoulders back and head high in his wide-brimmed traveler's cap and braided cloak, bag of necessities over his shoulder and knife at his belt. He'd waxed and polished his tall boots against the effects of rain and sun and wore an amulet at his neck his mother made to ward off evil spirits and traveling salesmen.

All the while, he struggled with the burning desire to run screaming from the village and never return.

A crowd began gathering, eyeing the heroes and talking in hushed tones. Some of the females, from budding girls to withering crones, giggled and waved at Flap, winking and making gestures that promised him a universe of perverse pleasures on his return. He acknowledged these with the grace of a chaste knight; only once did he lean back, point to his prominent codpiece then to each girl and woman in turn, drawing squeals of anticipation from all.

A sudden cymbal crash silenced the crowd and drew every eye to the huge double doors of the Village House as they opened. Through them came the cymbal crasher, a young boy dressed as an acolyte of Luddism in his pink dress and face veil, bashing two large brass plates together to call down the blessing of the Gods, quiet the crowd, and annoy everyone in attendance.

Following came the Baradan high priest of the holy church. The old man's white hair fell as low as his knees and provided the only cover for his backside, while a simple white sock tied around his loins housed his manhood below his long, white, wispy beard. The only other adornment was the tall, pointed hat of white, bearing in pink pictographs the ancient name of Ludd, ANSELSAM. Fingers up his nose and slapping his forehead, the priest loudly, if nasally, recited the old prayers and blessings and made his way toward the village center.

Following the priest came Gustall, the Chief Magistrate of Barada, in full ceremonial robes of bright yellow silk embroidered with colorful motifs of tree cats and rock snakes and extremely ornery weasels. His chain of office glistened in the early light as he followed the procession toward the well, smiling benevolently on the villagers who, by law and under threat of penalty, clapped and shouted his praises.

As the commotion reached a crescendo, the cymbals crashing, the priest emoting, and the crowd cheering, Oben heard the voice of fear in his heart say, "Now! Run!". But he spied his parents in the crowd. His father's look of pride and his mother's teary try at bravery planted his feet in the ground. When Gustall reached and climbed onto the small dais to speak and raised his arms, everyone fell silent, and the moment passed.

"Good people of Barada" Gustall began, "We are gathered today to celebrate two auspicious occasions. First, we are sending three of our bravest men on a vital and dangerous mission. Oben, son of Crent the Blacksmith and Tulee the Spunner, has agreed to lead this expedition that will bring great honor and possibly lucrative, renewable contracts to our humble village. Hip, Hip!"

The crowd responded with a legally mandated "Hooray."

Gustall pointed and went on, "Accompanied by his friends, Flap the Archer and Dongle the... uh... whatever he is..."

Dongle pressed one nostril and snorted, then the other, landing rock-sized expectorations on a nearby sleeping dog, then grunted, "Huhhehhuh. Booger."

"...uh, these three will deliver to King Otto a gift from the Grand Vizier, Zag..."

Gustall paused as three dozen foreheads received their protective slaps.

"... but entrusted to us to ensure prompt and safe delivery to our sovereign. This gift, this offering, is truly fit for a king, nothing less than a wonder of the world!"

He pointed to the rear of the Village House and bellowed, "Bring out Thunderhooves, the Magic Horse!"

"By Tyl's cock" Flap mumbled, "they couldn't have chosen a worse name if they'd held a contest."

A young boy led a horse by the halter from behind the house and walked it slowly toward the well.

Oben whispered, "Ludd's mercy on the poor creature."

The animal's back dipped like a wide bowl from withers to croup. Dirt and old sores mottled its white coat from lack of care. It worked its huge, flapping lips nervously, revealing pale gums and rotting teeth. The eyes traveled different roads, and the hooves tilted inward, the knees knocked, as if it had walked all its life in a gully.

The crowd fell silent. The horse looked over the gathering, snorted, and decided this was the perfect moment to lift its tail and, with a great, gaseous trumpet blast, dump a large, watery pile near the well, splashing onto Gustall's expensive slippers.

Unsure of the regulatory environment concerning humor at an official's expense, the crowd stifled their laughter and applauded, just to be safe.

The Magistrate shook his foot and approached the three men. "Oben of Barada, your people are counting on you to travel the perilous Forked Road..."

He again paused and joined the crowd in forehead slapping.

"...to deliver this wondrous animal to King Otto himself. At the village gate we have prepared a donkey-drawn cart full of provisions to aid and speed you on your journey. Do you accept?"

Gustall held out his hand in full expectation of a perfunctory clasp. Instead, Oben kept his hands at his sides, resembling nothing more than a small, frightened lapdog ready to bolt away.

Oben was again hearing the voice, repeating over and over, "Now! Last chance! Now!" He shivered and shook, his eyes unblinking, his mouth gaping open, not breathing.

A gasp from the crowd, followed by sighs of deep appreciation and then deafening cheers, broke the moment.

From the open doors of the Village House stepped Nios, her simple peasant skirt and blouse replaced with a stunning, full-length bridal gown of shimmering white. The high neckline and long, flowing sleeves guarded modesty, but the thin, clinging fabric served only to emphasize her voluptuous figure. She did not walk so much as flow over the ground, her body an arousing counterplay of rolling, shifting spheres. The mane of her shining black hair fell in cascading ringlets, framing her heart-shaped, unpainted face.

She approached her father and stood at his side, smiling and meeting every eye but Oben's.

Thunderhooves neighed loudly, pawed the dirt and threw his head. Flap smiled, tapped Oben and said, "Look at that!", pointing.

The stallion had developed a drop of epic proportions, a horse-cock for the ages, thick as a man's arm, purple with blood and flailing like a meaty club as the horse stamped and strained against the boy's tentative grasp on the halter. His eyes, wide and white, stared directly at Nios, his flaring lips and nostrils drinking in the ambrosial redolence of her allure.

Gustall saw nothing of the animal's rut. He beamed at his daughter and announced, "Here is our second blessing on this glorious day. At the strike of noon, my beautiful daughter Nios will wed Scut, son to Craps of Weewax..."

"The dung dealer?" someone laughed.

"Ahem" Gustall said, "Purveyor of fine, restorative mulch. And very, very rich."

Derisive chuckles rippled through the assembled.

"Come on out, Scut!" the proud father shouted, "and meet your lovely bride!"

A man, or a biped resembling one, stumbled down the Village House steps.

As he approached, all could see his clothing and accoutrements were of the most expensive variety but fit him too loosely here and too tightly there, as if assembled from random wardrobes. He limped as he walked toward the well, hiking his belt to keep his pants from falling and occasionally wiping his nose on his sleeve.

He took his place next to Nios, faced her father, and performed some distortion of his spotty face that seemed intended, to anyone's best guess, to approximate a smile.

Thunderhooves neighed and reared, kicking his front legs and waving his massive phallus in the crowd's direction like a cannon seeking a target. The boy struggled and was lifted off his feet when the animal reared, then stumbled when dropped to the ground. Men shouted, women and girls screamed, and all backed away from the now wild equine. The boy gave up and ran, leaving the horse to rear and kick with abandon.

Oben acted without thinking. He rushed to stand before the lust-maddened steed, arms at his sides, ignoring the flailing and stomping hooves mere inches away. He made no advance or retreat, settling himself in his body and heart as a source and beacon of calm.

Thunderhooves stopped rearing but still pawed at the ground and tossed his head. Oben stood stock still, his heart rate low and his breathing quiet.

Within seconds, the horse calmed and approached Oben. He nuzzled the man's shoulder and neck. When Oben raised a hand, Thunderhooves placed his muzzle in the offered, open palm.

Oben then drew a length of strong cord from his pack and tied it to the halter as a lead line. He faced the now-empty dais, and declared, "I accept!"

Cowering with the villagers some yards away, the magistrate murmured, "Hmmm? Oh, yes, I'd forgotten!" He did his best to gather dignity around himself like a cloak and strode toward Oben, extending his hand.

"Brave Oben, we of Barada entrust to you the fate of our fair village. Ludd speed you on your journey!"

As he clasped hands with Gustall, Oben glanced at Nios.

For the first time since her gentle kiss the previous night, she smiled into his eyes.

At the slightest tug on the lead, the horse moved forward at Oben's will. Flap and Dongle followed. The three men, leading the questionably supernatural horse, strode toward the village gate.

The crowd cheered without prompting.

Scut picked his nose and said, "Who wuz dat?"

Still watching Oben, a faint smile under her brimming eyes, Nios said, "My one and only true love."

Scut said, "Oh." He found what he sought deep in his nasal cavities, extracted and ate it.

Then he said, "Wait. Whut?"

Chapter 6 - It's Dangerous to Go Alone, Take This

A mile from the village gate, the companions arrived at the main crossroads and halted their tiny caravan.

To the left, the Mountain Road began its steep climb into the passes, rising and falling through a dozen villages on the winding way to Tamberlain. To the right, a lonely path led to the sea and the fishing villages along the Firth of Otto, renamed by long custom to honor the current sovereign. The change with each new king or queen confused postal delivery for a year.

Straight ahead began The Forked Road. It dipped downward sharply and disappeared into a dense copse of dark and gnarled oaks, thick with brittle, tooth-white alders and dense undergrowth. The bright light of late morning did not penetrate the canopy, as if Father Sun were too frightened to make visible what lurked there.

Oben stood at the head of his troupe, followed by Dongle leading the donkey, Flap riding the cart, and the horse following, tied to a stanchion. The jenny caught scent of what lay ahead and brayed. The horse likewise snorted and tossed his scraggly mane, pulling against the lead line and rocking the cart.

Oben hurried back to the frightened animal. "Steady boy, whoa, easy, shh."

The quieted equine nibbled at Oben's cap. He saved the hat and laughed, patting the horse's cheek. "That's a good boy, Thunder..."

Oben stopped short and said, "By Ludd, how I hate that name."

"Indeed" Flap said, "it's atrocious. Also, from what I've seen, it is false advertising. The only thing on this horse I'd describe as thunderous is his ass."

"Huhhehhuh" chuckled Dongle, "Thunderbutt."

Flap nodded. "That actually is much better. Certainly, more accurate."

"But it's not dignified" Oben said.

"Dignified?" Flap turned in the seat. "What of that poor, benighted creature would you say is dignified?

"He's just been neglected. Maybe abused as well." Oben moved slowly about the horse, touching, examining, assessing. "His teeth need floating, he should be fed more clover and less hay, a good farrier could straighten those hooves, and he needs about ten hours of brushing. I think if I worked with him for a few months, I could help him correct that sway."

"We have only three days" Flap said, "fewer if, as is likely, we get ourselves killed."

"I know. It's a pity. No horse deserves such treatment, only to be given to someone who will likely burden him under a heavy, armored saddle and spur him to charge into certain death."

Flap said, "But he's magic, correct? Guaranteed to carry King Otto to certain victory?"

"I doubt it. In fact, I'm afraid this might be some cruel joke Zag is playing on the king, and we'll be the ones to feel the brunt of Otto's wrath when he sees Thunder... I mean... dammit. What shall we call him?

"Thunderbutt!" roared Dongle, who then dropped his trousers, flexed his enormous, fleshy cheeks at his friends and let go a fart that echoed from the rocky slopes of Mount Tamberlain.

"By Tyl, he's got range" Flap said, holding his nose.

The horse suddenly tossed its head and let fly with a long, loud, lip-flapping neigh that ended in a majestic snort.

"Well, well" Flap said, smiling, "quite the singer, isn't he? A much better voice than any in that squealing chorus of chanters in church. Not that I go much, but a number of lovely ladies attend and so-"

Oben grinned and shouted, "That's it!"

"What is it?"

"His name. Chanter!"

The horse snorted and whinnied.

Flap said, "He seems to like it."

The horse nodded agreement and nuzzled Oben's shoulder.

Oben laughed, "Chanter it is, then."

Chanter lifted his tail and emitted a long, low vibrato, like an oboe warming up.

"Talk about talent" Flap said. "He can sing both coming and going."

"Thunderbutt!" Dongle cheered, hopping and waving his arms like a child with a new toy.

"Maybe he's magic, and maybe he isn't" Flap said, "but if we ever decide to take our show on the road, he must receive high billing. Chanter the Duet Singing Horse."

"Hehhuhheh" grunted Dongle, pointing at Chanter, "Chanter big peepee!"

Flap and Oben looked where the oaf pointed and gasped.

"The beast returns" Flap said.

The dark, massive phallus was again swinging below the animal's barrel, like the watch fob on a giant's vest, as he stamped and snorted.

Oben said, "Maybe the jenny's in heat."

The donkey dropped her ears, turned her head, and nervously eyed the rutting stallion.

"Ludd help her if she is" Flap said.

"Horse fuck! Horse fuck! Wanna see a horse fuck!" sang the jumping, smiling behemoth.

Chanter again pulled at the lead line, desperate to break free, throwing his head toward a nearby stand of trees.

Oben peered at the thicket. "Maybe he's scenting a wild mare."

"Or something more dangerous" Flap said, now scanning the area with a wary eye.

A low branch suddenly shook, as if a weight had landed, and the hissing yowl of a tree cat spooked men and animals alike.

In a single motion, Flap unshouldered his bow, nocked an arrow, drew, and loosed.

The missile whistled and disappeared into the thicket. At the scream of the cat, the archer nocked again and drew, ready for the charge of a wounded predator.

The cries of the suffering cat changed, softened, then resolved into the mewing of a kitten. As five sets of ears listened in wonder, the kitten transformed into a human, a woman's voice sing-songing, "Mee-ow, mee-ow. I'm just a poor widdle pussy cat wost in the scary woods. Pwease don't hurt me mister bad man."

The voice then fell into unrestrained laughter.

Flap eased the bowstring, smiled at Oben and said, "Definitely something more dangerous."

The bushes rustled again and parted, revealing Nios in her pure white wedding gown, now muddy at the hems. Her jet-black ringlets had lost their spring and dangled over her eyes, decorated here and there with leaves and moss.

She smiled and waved, shouting, "Hello the camp! Who's at home?"

Chanter reared and bucked, threatening to drag cart and donkey and archer with him as he struggled to reach the lovely woman in white.

Oben tried and failed to calm the stallion, so he quickly untied the halter lead to release him. Chanter trotted to Nios, head and tail high, his pride and joy bouncing and slapping his belly.

When he reached her, Nios cooed and petted his muzzle and cheeks. The great animal nickered and nuzzled her.

She pointed and shouted, "Well, somebody's glad to see me!"

Dongle suddenly shouted "Nios!" and ran to her, his steps thumping the ground like a charging bull.

Oben shouted, "Look out!"

Flap shouted, "No, boy! Down Dongle!"

As the massive man was about to tackle Nios, Chanter suddenly sidestepped, and body checked him with his massive rump. Knocked off his feet, he tumbled sideways down a hill and past the thicket of trees until he splashed unceremoniously into a small, babbling brook.

The men, the woman, the horse and even the jenny broke out in unrestrained laughter.

Dongle sat up in the chilly water, a slight gash on his forehead dripping blood down his bulbous, smiling face. He gurgled with laughter and began splashing himself and rubbing his armpits and crotch in a mime of bathing.

"Dongle wash!" he chortled. "Then Dongle boom-bam Nios!"

"You better wash well" Nios shouted at the splashing man. "You stink worse than the horse!"

"Yeh!" he shouted back, "Dongle wash!" His efforts redoubled, but his hands remained mostly in his groin. "Hehhuhheh" he grunted.

Nios led the still priapic stallion toward the cart, saying, "Truth be told, I'd rather boom-bam the horse."

Flap laughed, "Excellent! Another act for the road show."

She reached the cart and tied Chanter to the stanchion, then faced Oben, hands on his hips and brow dark.

"What are you doing here?" he said.

"I'm coming with you."

"No, you are not."

She pointed at her delicate nose. "Look at this face, Oben. Do you recognize this face?"

Oben said nothing.

"You know this face well. It's the face of me doing exactly what I mean to do. And this face is saying I'm going with you."

"It's dangerous."

"*I'm* dangerous."

"You're to be married."

She scoffed, "To that cull? Not on your life."

Oben's eyebrows raised in surprise. "But you told me last night that you would marry Scut."

"I said I'd marry him if you refused this challenge."

"So, you knew I'd accept?"

"No" Nios said, dropping her gaze and frowning, "I wasn't sure. I was afraid you might give in to the coward in your heart and refuse."

"But if I had refused, you would have married him?"

"Oh, Ludd, no!"

"But you said..."

Nios took a turn frowning and standing with her hands on her wide, curvaceous hips. "Did you see that excuse for a human?"

Oben nodded, "Yes, but..."

Nios shivered. "Ugh, never."

"Then, what?"

She shrugged, "I guess I would have taken up residence in the Dog and Duck, sucking and fucking and frotting every man, woman and mammal in the land. At least until you came home."

"What?"

"A girl needs a hobby."

"Dongle clean!" shouted the two-legged steer.

All watched him struggling to climb the hill.

Nios grabbed Oben's shirt collar and pulled his face close to hers.

"Listen to me" she whispered. "I left that abomination behind, along with my father, the priest, and all of Barada. I did it to be with you. Are you going to send me back? Now?"

Gazing into her deep green eyes, a vision crowded Oben's inner eyesight, a faint scene of bright light and clouds. The ears in his heart that hear no sound reported words from an unfamiliar voice he recognized in his bones:

I will make you marry me.

"No" he said.

"No?" Nios said, her face a mosaic of puzzlement. "No, you won't send me back or No, you won't let me come with you?"

"No" Oben said, "You won't make me marry you."

Nios frowned, then smiled, her eyes wary as if she'd heard something he'd said before, long ago.

She said, "I guess time will tell."

When Dongle reached the cart, he was breathing heavily.

"Tired" Dongle panted, unable to preface his remark with his name.

"No time for being tired" Oben said. "We're due in Tamberlain in three days."

He led Nios to the cart and helped her into the seat next to Flap.

Oben the blacksmith slapped his mighty friend Dongle on the shoulder and pointed him to lead the donkey.

Then he walked ahead, the first of his companions to set foot onto The Forked Road.

Chapter 7 - Hump or Death

Beyond the first patch of dark forest, the heavy canopy opened and bright sunlight in great beams poured through the branches, painting the path in mottles of gold. The warmth, the sense of adventure, and the lovely Nios by his side inspired Flap to tune his tonka and improvise a melody.

As he strummed and plucked the twangy instrument, he sang:
"A lad of Barada, adventure his game,
Left his village in search of his fortune and fame.
His lass, left behind, how she cried, and she pined,
While her friends gibed and teased her with questions unkind.
Singing' Hey, ho, where will you go?
Where will you go now your love's gone away?
She sang, hey, ho, to the bawd house I'll go,
There to service the lords and the ladies all day.
The lad, after three years, returned to his home,
Achin' to have his dear girl for his own.
But the woman at door was his lassie no more,
And he cried as her charity he did implore.
He sang, hey, ho, where did you go?
Where did you go while I was away?
She sang, hey, ho, to my bawd house, you know,
Where my girls serve the lords and the ladies all day."
Nios clapped her hands, laughing, and took over singing a coda:
"Hey, ho, where will I go?

Where will I go now my love's gone away?
Hey, ho, to the bawd house I'll go,
There to service the lords and the ladies all day."

"Hehhuhheh" grunted Dongle, "Nios boom-bam ladies."

Nios nodded, "Yes, indeed. They won't leave you with a babe in arms, they smell better, and their coin spends all the same."

Oben had dropped back to walk alongside the donkey, opposite Dongle.

"You wouldn't really do that, would you?" he said.

Nios grinned and said, "Do what, now?"

"What you said before, about the Dog and Duck."

"Service the lords and the ladies all day?"

Nios winked at Flap, nudging him with an elbow. He winked in return.

She said, "And what would you have me do, then, if not that?"

"Anything. Anything at all."

"Anything? Perhaps starve to death?"

"You wouldn't need to starve. There are many things you could do."

"Name one."

"You could be a spunner, like my mother."

"The word is *weaver*, and tell me, do you know of any unmarried weaver women in Barada?"

"I don't know. I could ask my mother."

She shook her head. "Don't bother. There are none. Do you know why?"

Oben did not answer.

"Because it is not a vocation. It's something married women do for their families."

"My mother sells some of her cloth."

"And who does the money go to?"

Again, Oben did not answer.

"Right. You know as well as I do. A woman marries, whores, or starves."

"What about the convent?"

"Ha! Whore myself to the priests with no pay and no freedom? Hard pass. It's the Dog and Duck for me."

After more silence, she said, "So, marry, whore or starve. Which would you have me do?"

Oben looked to the sky hoping the clouds might spell out the answer. He feared what the answer might be.

"Marry, of course."

"Oh? You did see the specimen my father chose, did you not?"

"Yes". He hesitated, then said, "He wasn't that bad."

"You marry him, then."

Flap and Dongle both laughed.

Dongle gurgled, "Hehhuhheh, Oben Boom-bam man butts."

Oben said, "You told me you could chase off any man your father picked for you. You said this one wouldn't last a week."

Nios sighed, "I know. I tried everything. I swore like a fishwife. I insulted him, laughed at his manhood, called him names in public and acted the shrew. He wasn't put off in the slightest. I would have to kill him to get away. That's only a temporary pleasure and bound to get a person talked about."

"But you were there, in your wedding gown," Oben pointed at the flowing dress, "That very gown, and your father announced your marriage."

"I was playing for time. Waiting to see what you'd do."

"And I did what you wanted. I accepted."

"Yes. And I was very happy, and very proud."

"Then, why-"

She shouted, "You left me behind! You just walked off. What was I to do? I'd rather whore than marry that walking stillbirth, and I'd rather be with you than whore. So, I ran after you."

Flap smiled but didn't meet Oben's glance. "Sometimes, dear captain, I wonder if your mother didn't drop you on your head when you were a tyke."

"So, those are my choices, Oben" Nios said, her eyes pleading, "You, or the Dog and Duck."

Before he could reply, a low growl from the underbrush ahead stopped the caravan. The jenny brayed and Chanter snorted, pulling at his lead.

Every breath stilled. The growling grew louder, more voices joining the chorus.

Flap stood in the cart, unslung his bow and nocked an arrow.

Dongle drew his club. Oben his knife.

Oben watched Nios hike her dress high, revealing a long, jeweled dagger hanging from a low-slung belt. She tied the hem of the dress to the belt and drew the blade.

Oben said, "You carried a dagger to your wedding?"

She smiled. "A girl on her honeymoon needs options."

The growling grew closer until a black muzzle baring long yellow fangs pushed its way through the undergrowth.

"Wild dogs." Flap said.

"Puppy!" chortled Dongle.

A second toothy snout appeared, then a third. The first crept closer, its enormous head now through the leaves, its yellow eyes focused and unmoving.

The other two emerged and followed their leader, a few steps behind and spreading out, their growling now accented with snarls.

"Only three" Flap whispered, drawing a bead on the first. "I can take two quickly."

A snarl behind the wagon spun the archer around to find two more black, growling curs creeping up on Chanter.

The horse stamped, pawed, and kicked; his eyes white with terror as he fought to escape.

"Apologies, lads" Flap said, "I can't shoot in two directions at once."

"Protect Chanter," Oben said, "Dongle. Spread out."

Oben gestured at the big man. They moved slowly left and right to draw the beasts away from the cart.

The two behind crept closer. Flap cursed, as Chanter was in the way of one shot, but the other was clear.

He aimed and drew, saying, "Give the word, cap'n."

Before Oben could answer, all five beasts moved as one.

The leader sprang for the jenny, but instead of attacking her throat, leapt onto her back.

The one close to Chanter did likewise, landing on the horse's rump and leaping at Flap while the leader bounded at Nios.

Flap's arrow pierced the first dog's heart, but the charging animal landed its full weight and sent the archer sprawling off the cart.

The leader aimed its jaws for the woman's throat, but she turned and drove her dagger between its ribs. The force carried her with it down to the floor of the cart, where she wrestled with the dog, thrashing and howling, spewing blood.

The other two attacked Oben and Dongle, leaping from the ground at whatever they could grip in their toothy jaws.

Dongle laughed, a child at play with a pet, and with a two-handed swing he batted the dog's head so hard the animal spun twice in the air before dropping, its skull crushed, twitching and gurgling.

Oben's foe knocked the knife from his hand and took him to ground but couldn't get purchase. Oben captured the dog's throat, throttling but not injuring the snarling, snapping canine. It stood on his chest, scratching with its long, sharp claws, lunging to bite at the nearest bit of flesh it could reach.

Oben grunted and growled back, cursing the dog and calling on Ludd for help.

As he was losing the struggle and the last of his strength, a vision appeared to him of an angel bursting forth from a vault of light in the clouds. The spirit of vengeance descended, her diaphanous white robe splattered with the blood of infidels, her face the visage of justice itself, the long blade of Ludd's righteous wrath raised above her head.

Nios screamed as she landed and drove her dagger into the base of the wild dog's spine. The animal's eyes went dark, and it slumped onto Oben's chest.

Before either could breathe, the last dog rounded the cart and sprinted for Nios.

Unable to pull her dagger free, she faced the onslaught and braced herself.

An arrow suddenly grew in the dog's eye, dropping him instantly to the ground mere feet away.

Oben and Nios watched Flap, standing on the seat of the cart, salute them with his bow and say, "By Tyl, that was fun! Let's do it again, eh lads?"

"More puppies!" Dongle yelled, running into the brush and swinging his club. "Here, puppy, puppy!"

Oben pushed the dead beast from his chest and sat up.

Panting, he said, "Thank you" to the smiling angel.

Her breath coming in quick gasps, she said, "Any time," and leaned toward him, her eyes glistening and her mouth parted.

Oben began to fall into the deep well of those eyes. He shook his head and suddenly struggled to his feet.

He shouted, "The animals!"

Flap was already calming the horse, checking for wounds. "Chanter's fine. Not a scratch."

Nios hurried to the donkey, nervously shifting in its harness and brayed quietly.

She called out, "She's all right, too."

Oben said, "None of them went for the animals."

Flap said, "Not your usual, run-of-the-mill wild dogs."

"This is not a usual, run-of-the-mill forest."

Dongle returned from the bushes and whined, "No more puppies."

"Thank Ludd" Nios said.

Oben stepped away from his friends and gazed down the Forked Road. Beyond the clear, bright patch where they stopped, the forest again grew heavy and dark. The road curved into the overgrowth and disappeared.

After a time, he said, "We should try to make the first fork before we camp. Agreed?"

Flap said, "Aye, cap'n."

Nios smiled and nodded.

The oaf laughed, "Hehhuhheh, Dongle go Nios."

Oben said, "Very well then."

The caravan reformed as before. Dongle and Oben with the donkey, Flap and Nios riding, Chanter bringing up the rear.

Blood spattered and breathless, no one cared to sing.

Chapter 8 - The Cock and the Crow

After an hour of silent travel, Nios cried out, "Ugh. I have got to wash some of this gore from me. I smell like a charnel house and it's making me sick."

"I hear a stream" Flap said, pointing, "It's down that gully a way."

"Then stop. I'm going."

Flap reined up the donkey, and the cart came to a creaky halt. Nios jumped down.

"Wait" Oben said, "It's not safe."

"That's why you're coming to guard me."

"What? I, no, uh, Flap? Go with her."

"The animals need watering" Flap said, stepping down, "You go."

"But I, oh. I... uh-"

Nios ran down the gully, her gown flying in the breeze, "Make up your minds, boys. I'm not waiting."

She disappeared behind a stand of trees.

"Flap? You go."

"I told you, cap'n, Chanter and the jenny need water. You go."

The oaf grinned and chortled, "Hehhuhheh. Dongle go."

Flap and Oben shouted "No!" in unison.

Flap took a bucket down from the wagon and began ladling water from the barrel.

He said, "Dongle. Dogs. Watch."

The big man drew his club from his belt, slapped it against his palm and scanned the area, grinning.

"Puppy? Here, puppy, puppy, puppy."

Flap filled the bucket and carried it to the donkey, not looking at Oben.

"Every man in the brigade has his task" he said and cocked his head toward the stream, "Yours is down there."

Oben hitched his belt and made his way through the underbrush, downhill toward the stream.

He caught up to Nios just as she reached a small, craggy rock face over which splashed the icy stream in a gentle but constant rush, filling a deep pool. He stopped, out of breath, a dozen yards behind her. She pulled the gown over her head in one swift motion, tossed it into the water and paused at the bank of the miniature lagoon.

A few seconds eyesight gifted him a lifetime of beauty. A single still image burned itself into his brain, of her in the dappled sunlight, stretching herself to the sky as if in thankful prayer. Gracious calves and thighs rose to the sweep of wide, smooth hips, her long white arms outstretched and framing the cascade of liquid onyx pouring over her bare, white shoulders. The thin leather belt surrounding her muscled waist painted the artist's masterstroke that drew the observer's eye to the taut, rippling dome of her haunch. The dagger and small purse tied at each hip imbued a dangerous, mythical tang, like incense, to the tableau.

He'd seen ancient carvings of goddesses, amalgams of beauty and terror, and understood at last what the artists sought to capture in wood and stone.

The portrait of Ludd's handiwork remained in his mind long after she had immersed herself. Shivering and laughing at the cold, she settled down and dropped her now drenched gown on a nearby rock.

When she spied Oben, she called out, "Come on in. You stink too."

"I'll stand guard."

"Keep your knife on you. I have mine. Nothing will hurt us."

"Five dead demon dogs back there on the road tell me otherwise."

"We'll be quick".

"They'll be quicker."

"Damn you, Oben. At least come over here and keep me company. If I was attacked by some bewitched rabbit right now, you'd never reach me in time, and it would rip my head off."

He made his way to the side of the pool and leaned against the curvaceous trunk of a willow. The branches shaded the pool and dangled delicate strands of leaves over the rippling water.

She took up her gown and scrubbed it in the flowing stream, rinsing away what did not permanently stain the fabric.

"Honestly, Oben, I don't understand you at all. Why do you hate me?"

"I don't. You know that."

"Yes, I do, but you make me suffer so."

"Me?"

"Yes, you. Leaving me behind with that shit-brain, Scut. How could you?"

"But what could I have done?"

She stared at him with wide eyes, "Are you as dense as Dongle? You could have grabbed me by the hand and dragged me away like a rapacious pirate."

"Your father would have called the village guard on me. You were betrothed."

The wide eyes narrowed, her lips tight, "You wouldn't have fought guards for me? You'd have me join myself to that... that... thing?"

"Dammit, Nios, you call me dense? Where would we be right now if I'd done what you say? We'd be on the run, every soldier in the county after us. Is that the wedded bliss you want? Is that life, to run and hide from the world, without home or family, without a country?"

The shimmer in her eyes rivaled the pool. Her chin quivered, but then he saw her jaw set, as if she'd willed her heart to cease its ache.

"You don't understand something very simple, dear Oben. If we were married, I'd live ten lifetimes in Tyl's Inferno or die at the gates of Ludd's Castle. I'd run and I'd hide and I'd fight and I'd lie and cheat and steal and do anything needed to be with you."

Oben opened his mouth to speak, but his lips knew no words.

"And I can't understand why you don't feel the same."

"I do."

"Then prove it."

She stood, her breasts dripping water, and stepped toward the edge.

Oben watched until the jewel of her navel appeared, then turned away, setting his forehead against the trunk of the tree.

"Yes," he said, his voice shaken, "we should go. It's time to go."

He glanced back as she stepped from the pool, then turned away again. "Yep. It sure is time to go. Where's your gown?"

She reached and enfolded him in her arms, pressing her body against his back like a wave reaching the shore, first her breasts, then her belly, then her hips and legs. She soaked his clothes with the cool stream water, but the feel of her flesh against him was warm as a campfire.

"Where's your gown?" he whispered, gritting his teeth.

She reached low and pressed her hand against his cock, already rigid. "Touch me, Oben, please."

He groaned, unable once again to turn away, to push her from him, to say no. Her hand gripped him firmly, squeezed and released, and squeezed again.

"I want you in me" she breathed into his ear.

"We're not married."

"We don't have to be."

"Yes, we do."

She squeezed him again. He felt his nethers tighten in anticipation.

With a smile in her voice, she cooed, "This big beauty belongs in me, Oben."

She pulled the top of his trousers out from his belt and down, found his cock again, now naked and free, and stroked it slowly, firmly.

"I..." he struggled, "I..."

With her other hand, she clutched his hair and turned him roughly to face her. Driving a deep-tongued kiss past his teeth, she found his cock again and squeezed him harder, moaning into his throat.

His knees weakened. He steadied himself against the tree and began responding, his hips pushing toward her.

"No," he cried against her lips.

She pulled her head back and groaned, "Aagh! Then touch me, Ludd damn you, touch me that way you have. You bastard, touch me!"

She clasped his hand and forced it between her thighs, found and guided his finger to her cleft and pushed him deep within. She bucked and ground herself against him, still pumping his manhood with greedy fingers.

He took over from her insistent hand and encircled the center of her delight with two strong fingers, spinning one way, then the other, until he heard her whimper, then pressed both inside her.

"Oh, Tyl's cock and balls" she swore, "I don't know what god or demon sired you, but your hands are a gift from the Great Provider himself!"

For a time, there was only the rushing stream, the groans of man and woman, the pressing and pushing and pulling of strong but tender flesh, and the faint breeze rustling the delicate tendrils of the willow, carrying the scent of pollen.

She suddenly shook, her body convulsing from belly to toes, hips to her head. She thrust herself wildly against his hand, took his shoulder in her mouth and cried openly in great heaves. Her teeth dug in, drawing blood.

She continued to work him. He felt the sap rise from deep below. She sensed the change in her hand and recovered, now pumping him in her fist, taking his sack in her other hand, pulling and squeezing.

"Mine" she growled. "Give it to me, damn you. Now!"

He froze, breathless, face turned to the heavens, eyes pressed shut. She grinned in triumph, watching as she milked a great geyser of cum from him, arcing to paint her breasts, cascading down her belly to mingle with the dark, sleek hair covering her mons.

"Yes, that's it" she purred, still squeezing and pulling, "That's my love. All of it, darling. All of it." Under her slowing but not easing grip, the fountain ebbed its last, thick gushes of his essence pouring over her hand.

They remained locked together, his fingers still in her, her hand still encircling him, kissing slowly, deeply, quietly, leaning against the tree, together, alone in the world.

"Oh, for Tyl's sake!" screeched a high-pitched voice. "Would you please just fuck the girl, already?"

Oben pulled Nios behind him, drew his knife and shouted, "Who's there? Show yourself."

From somewhere above, the voice said, "Ludd's nutsack, man, would you do yourself and me a favor and just split her slit with that ramrod of yours? I've got blue balls watching you!"

Nios caught sight first and pointed.

"It's a crow" she said.

Oben gaped, "A crow?"

The large black bird took three hops along the branch in the willow and cocked its head to regard the couple with one large black eye.

"Raven" it said, "I'm a raven, not a crow. Can't you tell?"

"Nios said, "Sorry, but for a moment you looked-"

"Yeah, bitch, we all look alike, huh?"

It hopped again and flapped its large wings. "Gods! Have you never traveled out of your village? Seen the world? Can't tell a raven from a crow?"

Nios grinned, "I didn't mean it like that, I..."

"Who are you?" Oben asked.

"I used to be a man, a scholar, an alchemist. Now I'm a raven. Go figure. You can call me Caw."

"What are you doing here, Caw?" Nios asked.

"Well, I *was* about to enjoy the Corvus equivalent of blowing my load, but you two just left me with dry nuts."

"That's all you were doing?" Oben said, finally belting his trousers, "Spying on us?"

"Well, no. Not at first, anyway."

"Then what?"

"I was sent to tell you Fil's coming."

Nios said, "Fil?"

"Yeah. The fucker who turned me into a crow."

Oben said, "Raven."

"Same, same."

Chapter 9 - The Wizard of Fuckall

Tired after a long day's labor, Father Sun made his way toward home behind Mount Fire as the tiny caravan moved on, bound to reach the First Fork before nightfall.

Caw, having lighted on the donkey's withers for the duration, regaled the companions with story after story about the wonders of being a bird. All the stories told of the same wonder.

"It's the flying" Caw said for the hundredth time, "That is absolutely, hands-down, or wings down I mean, absolutely the best thing about being a bird. Truly, cross my little black heart, of all the things that are great about it, the cawing, the eating roadkill, the cawing, flying is the best, the dog's bollocks, the bee's knees, the cat's pajamas. I mean, you can't conceive of how amazing it is to fly, at least I couldn't when I was a man, and I was a pretty smart guy, but I couldn't imagine in the slightest just how magnificent it is to fly. The flying is the greatest. Did I tell you about the flying?"

"Yes, you little boil on Tyl's bum" Nios grumbled, "You've told us about the flying for miles now."

"How about you do some of that wonderful flying?" Flap said, "and for the sake of Ludd, leave us alone."

"I can't, more's the pity. I'd love to do some flying right now, 'cause it's the best thing about being a bird, any kind of bird, really. I mean, being a raven is great because of all the cawing and the roadkill besides the flying, but even being a tiny sparrow would be beyond belief, crazy-ass wonderful, just because of the flying. Of course, I imagine being a huge eagle might be even better, floating on the currents and flying without so much as a wing flap. Wow, that could be even more amazing than being a crow."

Oben said, "Raven?"

"Same, same."

"Why?" Flap asked.

"Why what?"

"Why can't you do some flying and fuck off?"

"Fil told me I had to stay with you to make sure you reach the First Fork."

Oben said, "Why wouldn't we reach the First Fork?"

"Well, the wild dogs for one."

Flap said, "We already killed the wild dogs."

"You did?"

"Yes" Nios said, lifting a sleeve of her gown, "See all this blood? Wild dog blood."

"Wow. I thought you were just having a heavy month."

She turned to Flap. "Can you pick him off from here, without hitting the jenny?"

He drew his bow and an arrow from his quiver. "She won't even flinch."

Caw hopped and batted his wings, "Hey, hey, hey! Wait a fucking minute! "I'll be quiet, I swear."

Flap drew the string. "You'll be an appetizer by the campfire tonight."

The big man giggled, "Dongle want bird feet soup."

Oben held up a hand. "Don't."

"Can I just wing him?"

"No. He belongs to this Fil, whoever he is."

Caw stopped ducking behind his wing and screeched, "Hey, I do not belong to Fil you wanker!"

"I am not a wanker."

"You wanked your girl. Your girl wanked you. That makes you both wankers."

"Wanking" Flap said, "is when you do it to yourself."

"Spoken like an expert, pud-puller."

Flap kept his bead on Caw's head. "Just give the word, cap'n."

"No. Much as I'd like to see him skewered and roasting-"

Caw gasped, "Damn, that's cold, man."

"...we don't know who this Fil is, and he could want his crow back-"

"Raven!"

"...and he might be dangerous."

"Oh yeah, assholes" Caw cawed, "he's dangerous as fuck. He'll gut you all and make castanets out of your testicles already."

The bird pointed a shiny black wing at Nios. "You, pretty tits, he'll keep for kitchen duty and blow jobs."

Nios said, "Give me the fucking bow."

Oben pulled on the donkey's harness, stopping the cart, and yelled, "Everybody, quiet!"

He jabbed a finger at Caw. "If you don't want to be the first course tonight, then shut up about flying and wanking and tell us who Fil is."

"Okay, okay, keep your tadger in your pants, tosser."

"Flap?"

The archer drew the string taut. "Roast crow, comin' up."

"Wait, wait, wait! Look, Fil's not dangerous, not to you people, anyway. He wants you to get through this with your skins on. That's why he sent me."

Oben nodded. Flap let the string grow slack, but kept the arrow nocked.

Nios scoffed, "Why you? A scrawny little magpie."

"You, pretty tits, have a cruel streak."

"Flap?"

"I can see the future!"

Oben said, "The future?"

"Yeah."

"Then tell me what's going to happen."

"When?"

"Say, tomorrow?"

"I can't see that far."

"How far can you see?"

"Not far."

"Flap?"

Caw pointed a wing at Dongle and shouted, "He's going to fart!"

Everyone looked at Dongle.

The oaf grinned.

"Right about... now!"

Dongle let loose a long note, a basso profundo rising in a slow glissando toward tenor, his grin tightening as he squeezed the last fetid air from his great bellows.

"Hehhuhheh. Dongle hold that in too long."

Nios said to Caw, "You mean you can see only... Oh! Tyl's asshole!" She coughed and jumped from the cart, hiking her dress and running headlong past Chanter.

Flap dropped his weapons and did the same.

Chanter, tied in place, reared and neighed.

Oben looked at his companions and said, "What?" before he suddenly choked and followed.

The jenny seemed unperturbed.

Caw, meanwhile, had launched himself into the top branches of a nearby tree.

"Told you!" he screeched.

Rubbing his burning eyes, Oben approached the cart slowly and said, "So, you can tell the future, what? Ten seconds ahead?"

"Give or take five seconds" Caw said, dropping back down to land on the donkey.

"How is that useful to us?"

"Well," Caw ruffled his wing feathers and smoothed them with his beak, "If you'd run when I said, you would have avoided the stench."

Nios returned, fanning her face with her hand. "Useless" she said, "I vote crow's feet soup."

Caw turned one black eye on her. "Like the ones around your eyes, you old crone?"

Nios drew her dagger. "That's it. Die, jackdaw."

He escaped to the tree again. "I can talk, Ludddammit! Isn't that magic enough for you people?"

Oben said, "So what?"

"If you thought about it, clit-flicker, you'd figure it out. Remember the flying?"

Flap grabbed his bow from the cart, nocked an arrow and aimed. "Say 'fly' one more time pie-filling! I dare you. I double dare you!"

Caw hopped and flapped, "A bird who can talk. Put it together, people, this ain't alchemy."

Oben held out a hand, stopping Flap from loosing at Caw.

He said, "So, you could fly ahead, come back and warn us of danger?"

"Give the man a tankard of ale" Caw warbled, "he's won trivia for the night."

Oben, Nios and Flap looked to each other, nodding. They glanced at Dongle.

He frowned and crossed his arms. "Dongle want bird soup."

"Three against one" Nios said.

Caw hopped on the branch and cawed, "Four to one if you count me."

"We're not" they all said.

"All right" Oben said, "if you're really going to help us, you can stay."

Caw flitted down to his spot on the jenny's back.

Nios said, "So, who's this Fil?"

"Fil is the Wizard of Fuckall."

Flap said, "Wizard?"

"More of an enchanter, ask me, but hey, he's the one turned me into a raven, so who am I to judge?"

Oben said, "If this Fil is the Wizard of the entire Forest of Unholy Creatures Killing All Loitering Luddians, then he has to be one of the Unholy Creatures. Why does he want to help us?"

"To foil the plans of that evil wankstain, Grand Vizier Zag."

Chanter reared and neighed.

The four companions slapped their foreheads.

Caw said, "You know that superstitious shit doesn't work, right?"

Nios shrugged, "Habit."

Flap said, "Can't hurt."

Oben thought a moment. "If Fil wants to foil the Grand Vizier, then he wants us to fail. This horse is a gift from the Vizier, and we're taking it to King Otto."

"Yeah" Caw croaked, "we know."

"Then what does he want with us?"

The bird flapped his wings and shook his head. "You can ask him yourself. He's here."

All four companions grew wary, scanning the deepening shadows closing in on the road.

Oben said, "Where?"

"There" Caw pointed a wing to a nearby oak tree.

"Behind the tree?"

"No, stink fingers. He *is* the tree."

As they watched, the tree bark near the ground began shifting, flowing as if liquid, until the vague outline of a face formed. Then a body, short and squat, appeared below the face, followed by stubby arms. The animated body of oak bark stepped forward, leaving the tree as it was, and approached the caravan. As it moved, the rough wooden texture of the face smoothed, taking on the sheen of flesh, still mottled gray.

The body transformed from wood to cloth, a dark black robe of heavy wool. The face finally resolved in color to that of an extremely old man, withered with wrinkles, but still animated with the faint hue of life, as if standing on the doorstep of death.

The little man finally shed all remnants of the tree and stood before them, his pate hairless, his ears and nose bulbous, his eyes twinkling like a proud thief.

"Hey there" he smiled and chortled. "How's everybody doing this fine evening? I would have shown up sooner, but I got stuck at the *branch office* and couldn't *leave*."

He threw his arms open as if waiting for applause.

The four companions stared, silent.

He whispered, "Caw?"

"Oh, shit! Sorry" cackled the bird. He threw his head back and sounded a note-perfect impression of the ageless drum-and-cymbal punchline accent.

"Pa-dum, tish!"

"Thank you, thank you" laughed the little man. "I'm here all week. Try your waitress and tip the fish."

Oben said, "Fil?"

"In the bark... I mean, flesh!"

"Pa-dum, tish!"

"Ludd's balls" moaned Nios, "I'd rather have the talking crow."

"Raven!"

Chapter 10 - A Short Game of Whack-A-Fil

"Sheesh" Fil sighed, "tough crowd. I know that you're out there, folks, I can hear you groaning."

Oben said, "You're a wizard?"

"Wizard?" Fil said, feigning surprise. "Why, no, I'm just a simple traveling salesman."

At the word, Dongle's face grew red, his mouth twisting into a snarl, brow furrowed into a chevron of anger. He drew his club.

"Saaalesmaaan?" he roared.

"Nice pet ogre you've got there" Fil quipped. "Is he for sale?"

"Saaalllle?"

"Does he know any tricks?"

Dongle suddenly rushed Fil, raising his huge club over his head, screaming, "Saaalesmaaan!"

Fil watched the charging bull-man with a bemused expression, hands held casually behind his back.

With a loud, incoherent grunt, Dongle slammed his club on the spot where Fil stood, as if to drive a four-foot spike into the ground with a single blow.

When it landed, Fil was a yard away, to the left.

"Missed" he said.

The enraged oaf growled and lifted the club again, hammering where Fil now stood.

The short, old man appeared a few feet away, still nonchalant and grinning mildly, as if humoring a child.

"Try again?"

Dongle did try again, seven more times.

After the last, he panted heavily and could barely lift his weapon from the ground.

Fil called down from a branch of the oak tree, "So, what's his problem? Mother raped by a salesman?"

"No" Oben said, "His mother *was* a salesman."

"Oh. Makes sense." He waved and called out in a singsong, "Hey beef-brain, is it sinking in yet?"

Oben said, "Dongle, he's not a salesman."

The enormous man heaved a great sigh and slid his club into his belt. "Still asshole" he grunted.

From higher in the tree, Caw screeched with laughter, "Got that right!"

"Careful, birdbrain" Fil said, then turned up on the ground again.

"How do you do that?" Oben asked.

"What part of *wizard* don't you understand, sonny? I think something, and it happens. It's a gift."

Nios asked, "Can you do anything at all?"

Fil leered at her and said, "I can do anything *you* want, honey hips, and some things you don't want but will enjoy."

"Pa-dum, tish!"

"Not now, Caw."

Oben said, "Caw told us you want to help us."

"That's right."

"Why?"

"Because you're being used by that goat fucker, Grand Vizier Zag."

Chanter reared and neighed.

Everyone slapped their foreheads, including Fil.

Nios said, "Caw told us the forehead slapping doesn't work."

"What does he know? He's a crow."

"Raven!"

"What do you mean, we're being used?" Oben said.

"You're delivering that horse to King Otto, right?"

"Yes. It's a magic horse."

Fil laughed, "Sonny, that nag is no more magic than your donkey."

"Magistrate Gustall said that if King Otto rides him when he jousts King Hod, he's sure to win."

Fil pointed and waddled over to Chanter. "Really? Have you looked at this pitiful thing? It's a wonder he can stay on his feet."

He reached up to Chanter, who bent his head, snuffled the old man's hand, and snorted his ease.

Oben said, "If it's a magic horse, I thought appearance wouldn't matter."

"Sheesh, have you got a lot to learn. Half of magic is appearance, sonny." He made his way along, mumbling and petting the horse's shoulder and ribs as he went, "I'd be surprised if this poor beast didn't just collapse as soon as that fat fuck Otto put a foot in stirrup."

"Then what could the Vizier be doing? The horse is his gift. If Otto fails, then everyone will know he's to blame."

Nios joined the two men and petted Chanter's muzzle and cheek. "If Otto fails, Tamberlain falls to Aflax. Hod is king."

"Exactly, gorgeous" Fil said. "The winner of the joust becomes king of both countries."

Nios nodded. "And if Zag has made a deal with Hod, then he becomes Vizier to Hod, and nobody challenges him."

Flap sat on the end of the cart and said, "But that means Zag is still Vizier to a king. What does he get out of it?'

"He's Vizier to a new country that's twice as big" Fil said.

Oben wore puzzlement on his forehead like a sign. "What does that get him?"

"Power, baby" Fil said, "two kingdom's worth. Sometimes, being the guy behind the throne is better than sitting on it. All the power, none of the horseshit."

"And with one move" Nios said, "That throne is twice as big."

"Beauty and brains" Fil said, waggling his non-existent eyebrows at Nios, "How about you dump this country bumpkin here and come live with me. Once you go Wiz, that's all there is."

Nios grinned and walked past Oben, her hips swaying more than needed, saying, "Hmmm, maybe if you're real nice to us, and help us stay alive through this, who knows?"

She reached Fil and ran her delicate finger in light circles on his bald crown.

He shivered and smiled, taking a deep breath and sighing it out. "Whoo boy. I think I just grew a foot..."

Caw, now lighted on Chanter's head, whispered, "Wait for it..."

"Or something else twelve inches long!"

"Pa-dum, tish!"

Standing behind Fil, Nios faked a hearty laugh, waving at the men to join in.

Flap caught on and laughed woodenly, nodding at Oben.

Finally, Oben understood and joined in.

The three companions laughed unconvincingly while Fil smiled and bowed.

Nios waved for Dongle to laugh. He kept his arms folded and whispered, "Asshole."

When they stopped, Oben said, "If we're going to foil the Vizier then, we need to take Chanter back to Barada, warn the king, and reveal Zag's plans."

"What plans, sonny?"

"The plans we just discovered."

Fill shook his head and tisked like a disappointed father. "We don't know yet if that's what he's doing. And if you go home without delivering, all that will happen is Otto will blame Barada for ruining his joust. He'll punish the town somehow and kill you and your friends here in ways slow, painful, and humiliating."

Nios said, "Zag will just claim ignorance and try again."

Fil nodded, "Right. And after you four are reduced to grease spots and bits of charcoal, he'll hire the next schmuck to carry out his scheme, and probably succeed."

Flap said, "So, we have to go along, reveal the plot, and stop it somehow."

Oben frowned. "How?"

"We figure it out as we go, sonny. And now you can't lose, with me on your side."

"Me too!" cawed Caw.

"Yeah, yeah" Fil said, waving the bird off, "if you can keep your beak shut for five minutes."

Nios smiled, "Your lips to Ludd's ears."

Oben looked to Nios, then Flap. "So? Are we agreed?"

Flap said, "Aye, cap'n."

Nios smiled and made her hip-swaying way to Oben. She held his arm in both hands and gazed into his eyes. "Wherever you go. I told you that already."

Fill fanned his face with his hand and said, "Sheesh! Is it hot in here or is it her?"

"Pa-dum, tish!"

Oben fought to turn away from the lovely woman and asked the big man, "Dongle?"

The oaf, still cross-armed and frowning, threw a two-fingered salute and farted.

"So, that's two votes for me?" Fil said.

Nios let Oben go and went to Dongle, chin down and holding his gaze under lidded eyes, her undulating walk and sideways smile an invitation to male desire as ancient as the orgiastic, world-creating gangbangs of The Old Ones.

"Dongle" she pouted, clasping his arm and whispering in his ear, "Dear. Sweet. Dongle."

The gigantic man's huge smile was matched only by the sudden, enormous bulge in his trousers.

Nios whispered something to the oaf the rest couldn't hear.

Watching this display of seduction, Fil whispered, "Holy horse hummus! I'm gonna need some virility spells just to hang out with you guys."

Dongle's eyes and grin grew impossibly wide. He began to chortle and nod his head at whatever promise Nios was making.

He suddenly grabbed his crotch and shouted, "Dongle go Nios!"

Nios leaned her head on Dongle's arm and smiled at Oben.

"It's a gift" she said.

"Very well" Oben said to Fil, "We'd better get moving. How much farther to the First Fork?"

"Farther? We're there."

Oben looked down the road. "What? I don't see it."

"It's behind us" Fil said, hooking a thumb over his shoulder, "Back there."

Oben, Flap, Nios and Dongle all craned to look down the road they'd just passed. Nothing was different.

"Oben said, But I-"

"Oh, sorry" Fil said, grinning and pointing, "I mean, it's that way."

The companions turned. The First Fork, just a dozen yards away, led off left and right at easy angles from the main road.

Everyone looked at Fil with mixtures of confusion and fear.

He said, "I goofed and said it wrong."

Oben said, "What?"

"I told you, I think something, and it happens. I thought, I really want to get *forked* by her, and here we are."

Silence and stares finally spurred Caw to action. "Oh, shit! sorry! Pa-dum, tish!"

Chapter 11 - Attack of the Thief Gnomes

Mount Fire glowed as it welcomed Father Sun's daily homecoming, lit first by his passing brilliance, then from the flaming, bubbling lava rising from the depths of Tyl's Inferno that eternally threatened to escape the crest. With the Father away resting, the playful children of the sky danced twinkling in the celestial sphere, their music and laughter a prelude to the nightly courtship about to begin.

While the others set up camp and started a fire, Dongle managed, splashing in the stream and growling bear-like, to capture a fish for each. Now, as dark descended, the companions sat on logs around the fire as the fish slowly roasted in an iron basket. Nios tore handfuls of dark, seed-filled bread and handed them around on wooden trenchers, while Oben cut wedges of hard, sharp cheese and Flap filled wine cups. They settled themselves with their first course and ate silently. The chirping of crickets and first hoots of owls riding on a whispering, pine-scented breeze served as the meal's musical accompaniment.

Tied to a nearby tree, Chanter and the jenny grazed contentedly on a patch of clover.

Oben used a leather glove to lift and open the basket, holding it as Nios added a fish to each trencher. Moans of delight rose to join the forest chorus as each picked at the delicate flesh.

Dongle stuffed the fish in his mouth, pushed the tail in with a finger and happily chewed.

After a few moments of quiet and sips of wine, Caw stopped pecking at the worms and grubs he'd gathered for his supper and suddenly said, "You know, another thing about the flying that I really love, I mean, maybe the best part-"

Five mouths shouted, "Shut up, Caw!" loud enough to silence the crickets and owls.

"Hey, I'm just trying to make conversation, here."

"Dongle still hungry" the oaf declared, eyeing Caw. "Dongle eat bird."

"Okay, okay!" Caw said and went back to picking at the insects.

Flap said to Fil, "I understand that the babbling bird here was once a man, an alchemist. Why did you change him into a crow?"

"Raven." Caw cawed.

"Same, same."

Fil smiled. "Well, unfortunately I can't tell you, because it was the result of a wager, and if either of us reveals what the wager was to anyone, that one loses the bet."

"Go ahead" Caw said. "Tell them. I won't mind."

"Ha, nice try you squawking squab. I'm going to win this bet, if it takes until the day Ludd evicts Tyl from the Inferno."

"In your dreams, short stuff."

"I can only tell you" Fil said to the others, "that there was a woman involved."

Nios grinned and eyed Oben. "There's *always* a woman involved."

Oben blushed and sipped his wine.

"You got that right, sweet lips. And thank the Gods for that. Just as Father Sun for all eternity encircles Moa, without the ability or the desire to escape, there is always a woman at the center of everything."

Flap raised his cup. "So it is, so may it always be."

Everyone, including Caw, repeated, "So may it always be."

Nios left her place and, with soft, slow steps, approached Oben and sat, bumping him with her hip to make room. She leaned against him and raised her cup.

"So may it always be" she said.

Oben touched her cup with his and they drank, their eyes mutual prisoners.

"Holy cock-stand" Fil sighed, "if you kids are selling tickets to this show, I'm buying."

"He's the shy one" Nios said, her eyes smoldering. "I'd take him right here and let the world watch for free."

"Well, well" Fil said, rubbing his hands together, "we've had dinner, time for the entertainment." He leaned forward, braced his elbows on his knees and set his chin in his hands, eyes wide and grinning.

Oben downed his wine and said, "What fork do we take?"

Fil shook his head like a man awakened from a dream. "Wha, what?"

"Tomorrow. Which fork do we take?"

Fil looked to Nios.

She said, "Told you."

"It's important." Oben said, "If we take the wrong fork, it might mean greater danger, or we get lost, miss the joust and the king kills us."

Fil sighed, "Some guys never take a day off."

The jenny brayed. Flap glanced over, but she seemed to settle. He opened the wine jug and began refilling cups.

Oben waved the wine away and said, "Well?"

"It's not that simple, sonny. Here in Fuckall, you don't just say the left way leads to this and the right way leads to that."

"Why not? Don't you know this forest?"

Fil frowned. "Don't insult a wizard, sonny. You get rotten wizarding."

Chanter nickered and stomped. Oben turned to watch the horse flap its ears and lips nervously, snort, then return to cropping clover.

"I know this forest better than anyone, so that's why I say it's not a simple choice. Fools who pass through here thinking there's one right way are the ones who never make it out."

Both the donkey and Chanter whinnied and stomped, waving their heads to pull at the ropes binding them to the tree.

Fil said, "The first thing to learn-"

"Fuck!"

Flap turned to peer into the darkness. "What in Ludd's name was that?"

Another scream came from the bushes opposite the first. "Fuck!"

Everyone stood, heads turning left and right, drawing weapons. Caw flapped his way to a high branch.

"Fuck!"

"Fuck!"

"They're everywhere" Nios whispered.

Fil shouted, "Quick, backs to the fire!"

The companions formed a circle around the campfire, taut and ready, watching, waiting.

"Fuck!"

Fil whispered, "Thief Gnomes."

Flap said, "Why didn't your craven raven warn us?"

From the top of the tree, Caw mimicked the five voices perfectly. "Shut up, Caw!"

"Point taken" Flap said.

With a sudden chorus of voices shouting, "Fuck!", five tiny men appeared from beyond the firelight. Nearly identical, each was barely two feet tall, with long white beards, belted blue jackets, trousers and boots. Their conical caps were of different colors, and each wielded a small but heavy-looking club.

"Hehhuhheh. Baby men!"

The red-capped gnome facing Dongle screamed, "Fuck!" and ran at the giant, swinging his club. As Dongle laughed, the gnome landed a hard knock against his shin. The big man screamed in pain, lifted his leg, and took a second blow to the other.

Dongle fell, fending off more strikes to his body and head from the stunted humanoid.

The other four attacked together, with a mighty shout, "Fuuuck!"

Flap's sword and bow lay in the wagon, and the approaching gnome in a green cap blocked his path. He kicked the tiny attacker, sending him yards away, but the growling, cursing creature recovered and ran screaming back to the fray. Flap drew a throwing knife and speared the raving man between the eyes, throwing him flat on his back and twitching with death throes.

Oben dropped to one knee and drove his knife into the blue-capped miniature monster coming for him, but took a knock to his head in the bargain. He recovered, pulled his blade from the gnome's heart and watched as he fell, gurgling and gasping.

The white cap attacking Nios threw away his club and jumped onto her leg, latching himself onto her like a monkey to a tree. He furiously humped her, eyes wild and screaming, "Fuck, fuck, fuck!"

She gripped his beard to yank his head up, slashed his throat with her dagger and flung him to the ground. She added a head stomp for good measure.

The moment Oben's gnome breathed its last, it disappeared in a puff of smoke and another blue-capped replica appeared a few yards away, screaming the same monosyllable and running at Oben with his club raised and fire in his eyes.

Dongle had meanwhile captured the red-cap gnome in his massive hands. With a mighty groan, he twisted the gnome's head and pulled it from his body with a resounding pop. He tossed the two halves away. The head lay gaping and the body running chaotically around, like a freshly butchered chicken.

In this time, Flap had used two more of his knives to kill two repeats of his gnome, each wearing green and each as ferocious and foul-mouthed as the first. Another simply appeared and took its place. Flap drew a small dagger, his last weapon, and braced himself.

Nios, too, had slit one more throat, and was driving her blade into the skull of another white cap as it tried desperately to climb her leg and finger her quim.

As with the others, Dongle's gnome puffed into nothingness and reappeared, resuming the attack.

The fight continued this way for a time, each of the four killing their respective foes and then continuing the fight against an identical replacement.

Only Fil held his own against the black-capped fighter facing him. Arms outstretched and face strained, he held the gnome at bay without touching him. Black Cap's face screamed his fury silently, his club raised, shaking with effort, but he could not break the hold.

Oben dispatched his fourth bluecap and shouted, "Fil! We can't keep this up. Help!"

"I'm workin' on it! Keep your shirt on, sonny."

Dongle had now crushed two gnomes with his club and was chortling like a boy playing with toys.

"Three" he laughed as he splattered the third with a mighty hammering. "Dongle do counting. Here, four!"

A fourth red cap obliged the giant. One sweep of the club reduced him to a pile of goo for his trouble.

Fil struggled to hold his gnome at bay as he took one hand away and pointed it in the other direction, shouting an incantation, "*Amoco ell overload!*"

A sparkling, shimmering bubble grew around Fil, extending outward, growing in width and height. It reached Dongle on his left and Oben on his right, and when their gnomes returned, they ran into the bubble as if into a wall. Hitting it with their clubs did nothing to break the shimmering dome.

The bubble grew, covering the campfire and then reaching Flap and Nios on the far side. Large enough for all, the weary fighters regrouped under its protection and huddled together around the fire, watching as the five Thief Gnomes tried hitting, kicking, and tearing at the protective shell to no avail.

Black Cap suddenly shouted, "Fuck!"

All the gnomes stopped and listened.

Pointing and saying *fuck* with twenty different inflections, Black Cap gave orders. As one, all five ran to the animals.

"Chanter!" Oben gasped.

Muttering and shouting, the gnomes went for the horse. Three formed a ladder to put one on his back while another untied his lead. The animal bucked the would-be rider off and kicked another into the bushes. But two held tight and pulled, leading him away.

Oben stood, "We've got to-"

"Hold on, sonny."

Fil pointed to Chanter and intoned, "*Ferrous hoy Ono!*"

Chanter vanished without the courtesy of a puff of smoke.

Everyone watched, smiling, as the five diminutive demons clambered and searched, *fuckfuckfucking* their way into a frenzy of confusion and anger.

Smiles melted into frowns and scowls as the gnomes turned their ire on the jenny, releasing her, taking hold of her lead and slapping her haunches.

They took her away, braying and crying, before anyone could say, *fuck*.

Chapter 12 - Magic Ain't Just for Wizards

Fil waited until the chorus of profanities died off in the distance before he removed their protective screen.

"*Be geed moon!*" he intoned, and the diaphanous shell faded away.

"Chanter!" Oben said, running to the thicket where the animals had grazed, "where is he?"

"Safe, sonny, fret not."

"You can bring him back?"

"You think I don't know how to reverse my own spells or something?"

"Well, I-"

"Kids today, I tell ya. No respect for their elders."

"Well, then? Bring him back."

"Heh, look who's in such a hurry, without even a thanks I get? Like maybe for saving everybody including the horse..."

Oben said, "Thanks, Fil."

Fil rolled his eyes. "Your enthusiasm is overwhelming."

"Yes indeed" Flap said, "we are eternally grateful for the brave and timely deeds of heroism and magic with which you pulled our dangly bits from the jaws of diminutive danger. Grammercy."

"Sheesh, condescension I don't need."

The oaf said, "Dongle thank asshole."

"Honesty. I like it."

Nios glided to the little wizard, grabbed him by the ears and planted a wet kiss on his wrinkled lips.

When they parted, she remained bent to him, patting his cheeks, so that her décolletage drew his eyes like a moth to a flame.

"Hoo, boy. Now that's how you say thanks, sonny. You could learn something from magic thighs here."

Flap said, "Upon the next adventure, we will all take turns giving you deep, appreciative tongue kisses."

Dongle coughed, hacked, and spat.

"And with that" Fil said, waving his arms dramatically, "*Horsehair Oases!*"

Chanter appeared, standing by Oben, and snorted a welcome.

Oben murmured reassurances and petted the great animal's forehead and cheeks.

Looking him over, he said, "I don't understand. He's... he is..."

Fil smiled, holding hands with Nios as they approached. "Eh, just a little extra something I threw in because of gorgeous here."

"He's lovely" Nios said and petted Chanter's neck.

The once sickly animal stood with a proudly straight back, head high, flaxen mane and tail long and healthy, his white coat smooth and hooves polished.

Oben stuttered, amazed, "How?"

"I told you. Think it, and it happens."

Oben went to the old man and took his hand. "Thank you, Fil, thank you so much."

Fil held Oben's hand and pulled him down to meet his eyes. "You're welcome. And remember, sonny. Think it, and it happens."

"But I'm not a wizard."

Fil winked, "Here's a little secret tip about magic. It's not just for wizards."

Nios braided Chanter's mane and said, "Looks like it's not just for humans either" and pointed.

Everyone stared at the animal's great phallus, in full bloom, swinging gently as Chanter stamped his back legs and nickered softly, his eyes on Nios, white with excitement.

"Holy stallion sheath!" Fil laughed. "You best take care, missy. You don't want him to mistake you for a mare."

Nios grinned, still working strands of Chanter's golden mane. "Hmmm, could you turn me into a mare, Fil, just for a time?"

Fil's eyes went wide. "Uh, yeah, maybe, I, uh... wow."

She met Oben's shocked face with a sly grin. "At least somebody would be honoring the joy I have to give."

Fil stood gaping a moment, then pulled Oben aside and whispered, "Word to the wise, sonny. You better tup that girl, and soon. I speak from experience. A woman like that won't wait forever, and she doesn't have to."

"But..."

"Remember what I said. Magic ain't just for wizards."

Oben glanced at her again, still holding his eye, her hands working strands of the silky mane, leaning her shoulder against Chanter's mighty neck.

The massive horse cock showed no sign of drooping.

Oben whispered, "Can you really turn her into a mare?"

"Sure. But so can you, if you know what I mean."

Oben caught Fil's wink and grin and smiled.

"Remember the old saying, sonny, he who hesitates is fuckless."

"Is that how it goes?"

"Close enough for government work."

The hour grew late. The celestial couple had already spoken their vows and were on their way to their honeymoon behind Mount Fire.

Flap took up the role of camp boss and organized the troupe to prepare for overnight. They gathered extra wood and stoked the campfire high and hot to ensure good coals. Dongle pulled the heavy cart nearer and tied Chanter there for close watch. Everyone stowed their belongings in the cart, tied down against a return of the foul-mouthed gnomes, or more stealthy thieves.

Gathered around the fire covered in blankets, they shared a small flask of brandy and listened, enraptured, as Fil told scary stories.

"So, three times the princess hears this terrible scraping sound on the side of the carriage. Now truly scared, she pulls the prince's hand out from under her skirt and demands they leave the grove. Poor boy prince has a whopping boner and begs her to keep rubbing him through his pants, but she orders the driver to whip the horse's eyes to get away fast. They race back to the palace in angry silence. He still plays the gentleman and gets out to open her door. When he does, she sees his eyes bug out and a terrible look of bone-chilling fright on his face."

Fil paused for effect, drawing out the reveal. His audience stopped breathing.

"There, on the carriage door, *was a bloody hook!*"

Everyone gasped and laughed, except Dongle, who cried into his hands and blubbered, "No hook! No hook!"

Nios went to the man-child and cast her spell over him, speaking a motherly lullaby now rather than a siren song. Soon he was smiling, and then laughing as she tickled him, ruffled his greasy hair, and returned to her place under the blanket with Oben.

Flap asked Fil, "Do you think those gnomes were working for Zag?

Chanter neighed and reared.

"I don't think, I know. They're mercenaries, taking any job that pays in coin, the greedy little cat fuckers."

Oben said, "They were obviously after Chanter."

Nios said, "But why did they attack us and not just sneak him away after we were asleep?"

"Two reasons" Fil said, "one, they're crazy as shithouse rats. Two, they wanted *you*, pretty puss."

"What?" Nios said, sneering. "wanted me? As in...?"

"Yep. By about now you'd be tied down and pulling a small but very enthusiastic train."

"Ugh!"

Flap said, "They didn't try to kill her, like they did us."

Oben's eyes narrowed as he clenched his jaw in anger. "You mean the Vizier was trying to kidnap Nios?"

Fil shook his head. "I doubt it. Not the type. All he cares about is power. He wanted the horse. The gnomes were just trying to get her as a bonus for themselves."

Nios said, "What can he want with the horse? We're expected in Tamberlain to deliver it. If we fail, doesn't he take the blame and lose favor with Otto?"

Fil sighed, "I wish I knew. It's got me bamboozled. All I do know is that we need to keep Chanter from him. It's got something to do with the joust, and nothing good, I'm sure. But he'll try again."

For a moment, all were quiet. They stared into the flames, and Fil saw in their faces the fear of what it might mean for the Vizier to try again.

Flap saw the change in his comrades too, and said, "Well, we better get some sleep. Dongle? First watch."

The big man stood and drew his club. "Dongle watch."

The rest bedded down around the fire, Flap and Fil on opposite sides, Oben and Nios blanketed together under the cart.

For a while, the quiet was complete. No crickets sang, no owls hooted; even the breeze seemed to have retired for the night.

Then, quiet words escaped the blankets and rose in the chilling night air. There followed suppressed giggles, and more words.

"Please!"

"No."

"Damn you, Oben!"

"Here, let me..."

The blankets shifted and tossed, the laughter melting into sighs, then moans.

Fil sat up, watching the now-living pile of cloth. He smiled at the spectacle of lust, seeing what they were doing in his mind's eye, drinking in the sweet nectar of their pleasure.

The blankets now jiggled and danced. Moans, sighs, and whispers grew insistent.

Fil finally noticed Dongle standing at the fire, staring at the couple. He held his massive manhood in one hand, club in the other. Soon he was stroking himself so hard the sound echoed through the forest, like a fighter practicing punches on a side of beef. *Whap, whap, whap!*

Flap came out of his blanket and whispered loudly, "Dongle, don't do it man! You'll put the fire out!"

Nios and Oben remained oblivious to anything but their enjoyment. As their thrashing reached a crescendo, Nios cried out, "Oh, Oben!"

Back arched, his cock cantilevered over the fire pit, aglow in the flames, Dongle's great, deep groan of his pleasure sounded.

"Dammit, man! Don't!" Flap pleaded.

Fil reached out his hand and whispered a spell, "*Avie freshet!*"

A small, sparkling dome, like the one that had saved them from the gnomes, covered the fire, just as Dongle held his breath and pumped out a massive cascade of man spunk. It arced and landed with loud splats on the protective shell, collecting in a thick and glistening ring around the stones of the fire pit.

The blankets slowed their movements. Satisfied sighs signaled the couple's own finish.

Flap smiled at Fil and said, "Grammercy, prince of wizards."

Fil nodded and laid back under his blanket.

From high in the tree, Caw cursed, "Luddammit! I'm never gonna bust my nut!"

Chapter 13 - Whose Donkey is That Donkey?

There was no joy around a similar campfire, some distance away in the cave of the Thief Gnomes.

Any mortal close by would have heard only a hundred variations of the word, *fuck*. Translated, the diminutive devils were grousing about the job gone wrong and, like most organizations run by committee, blaming each other.

"Fuck you" said Green to Red, "I took three knives to my noggin' and I still can't think straight. That shit hurts, asshole!"

Red shouted back, "You think I don't know it hurts? I had my head ripped off by that two-legged mountain! Then I was smashed like a bug maybe a half-dozen times. Don't tell me about hurt!"

White, his voice raspy and faint, said, "We should have just grabbed the horse and ran."

"Oh really?" said Blue. "Now you say that? Mister 'I can get the girl in two seconds' has changed his tune. We should've just taken the horse, he says. You promised us a pussy parade, cock-knocker!"

"How could I know she'd be such a killer bitch?" White coughed. "I thought she'd squeal and faint and I'd carry her off like nothing." He rubbed his throat and grimaced. "Anybody got a lozenge?"

Black shouted, "Shut up, all ya! It was that putz Fil who fucked things up for us. After he put them under that shield, we still couldn't grab the horse because he pulled some kind of mumbo jumbo. So, listen up, assholes, and listen good. Fil's the reason we failed. We don't need

Zag thinking it was us, or he'll cancel our immortality ticket, carve us up alive and eat us for lunch on toast points."

The gnomes all mumbled agreement and nodded.

"Okay, then," Black said, "let's get this over with."

The five took their places around the fire, forming a star. They closed their eyes and raised their arms.

"Vizier Zag" Black intoned.

"Come before us" cried the others.

"Great and powerful Zag" Black said, his intensity rising.

"Stand before us!"

"Vizier Zag!"

"Come before us!"

Their voices climbed, louder and higher, with every repeat of their summoning spell.

The flames responded, leaping, crackling, changing color from yellow and orange to red and blue. A figure formed — a man made of fire, translucent and flickering — growing more solid as the voices rose to screams.

"Great and powerful Zag!"

"Stand before us!"

The fire suddenly died, like a match blown out. In its place stood the infamous Grand Vizier Zag, tall and impossibly thin, his black silken robe flowing to his feet, embroidered with magical symbols in blood red. He stared into space through dark, heavy-lidded eyes, his gaunt, hollow-cheeked face impassive as a wax statue. A huge diamond, said to possess unimaginable power, pinned the black turban that covered his head.

Now gripped with the fever of their enchantment, the gnomes howled their call.

"Vizier Zag!"

"Come before-"

"Enough!" screamed the magician, his voice shaking the cave walls. "Silence, you hideous horde of homunculi!"

The gnomes quieted and stepped back, shaking with terror.

"We're sorry, your ickiness" pleaded Blue.

White whispered, "Deepest apologies, oh, loathsome lord."

"Mercy upon us" cried Red. "we are but poor-"

Zag reached out his open hand toward Red and suddenly closed his fist.

Red's body collapsed on itself, as if crushed by a giant. His bones crackled and crunched while his entrails escaped in oozy rivulets. He gurgled his last breath, vanished and reappeared a few feet away from the fire ring.

"Ouch" he said.

Zag glared at each gnome and then hissed, "Much better."

Tied up near the cave entrance, the jenny brayed.

Zag gazed at the animal for a moment, his face drooping into a frown.

"Tell me" he said slowly and quietly, "Whose donkey is that donkey?"

The others all looked to Black, their leader, to answer.

"Well, um" he stuttered, "your darkness, your badness, your evil sliminess, you see, it's like this"-

Zag held up his palm, making Black flinch.

"Speak my language, if you please. I can't make out any of your *fuckityfuck* talk."

"Oh, right" Black said, switching to the unfamiliar tongue of mortals. "Like this, is it, sir, madam, sir." He pointed, "Animal big ears from come peoples attack we did at camp. Tonight. That when."

Zag sighed, "You haven't been practicing, like I ordered, have you?"

"Not."

"Gaining the ability to speak to me in my language was one condition for the immortality I granted to you tiny twits, was it not?"

"Was, it was" Black said, searching his limited vocabulary, "Learning to practice we should, and not, did, but now try tomorrows, ever."

"Very well" Zag said. "Now tell me, where is my horse?"

"Horse. Not is here."

"I can see it not is here, you half-pint half-wit. Where is it?"

"Poof."

Zag glared down at Black, holding the gnome's gaze. Without a word, Black began shaking, then choking and gurgling until frothy saliva flowed from his clenched lips. His eyes bugged and his face turned redder with each second until Zag turned away. Black fell to his knees and gasped for breath.

"Please" Zag said through an evil grin, "do go on."

"Horse" Black gasped, getting to his feet, "magic. Poof did thing, then not."

"That horse is not magic, mini moron. Not until I put a spell on it, in any case. That's why I need it here. Now, let me try again. Where. Is. My. Horse?"

Black finally found his breath and said, "Fil."

The Grand Vizier of Tamberlain stared at the far wall of the cave, motionless, his face blank.

The gnomes closed their eyes, bracing for punishment.

Zag finally drew a deep breath and sighed it out.

"Fil, you say?"

"Yes. Thing Fil do, horse not."

The magician pondered a moment, tapping a finger on his chin. "Hmmm, tell me, why did Fil know you were there? You are the Thief Gnomes. Known for stealth. You've stolen hordes of gold from under the watchful eyes of alert guards. Virgins from their convents. Babies from their mother's arms. What made stealing a horse from a collection of village dolts so difficult?"

The five thieves glanced nervously at each other, searching for the right victim to blame.

Black said, "Woman."

Zag regarded Black as he would a fly landing in his porridge. "Woman?"

Red suddenly pointed to White and shouted, "Idea him woman take we! Him, him, him!"

White turned on Red. "You backstabbing little shit-stain! I'll carve your heart out with a spoon! I'll-"

Before he could speak his next word, White burst into flames. He ran a lap around the fire pit, then sprinted, shrieking in agony, through the cave entrance and into the forest.

After a time, when the screams had died off in the distance, Zag said, "I believe I said no more fuck talk, did I not?"

The gnomes nodded and mumbled agreement.

"Very well. Now, what about a woman?"

Black struggled to explain, "Woman, have they and, um, beauty wow very." He held his hands out from his chest, "These, like, yes much and..." he put his hands on his hips and swayed side to side, "bum, bum, bum... like we idea take and keep at cave and do..." he thrust his pelvis forward and back, "do lots like in-out-in-out this."

He paused, looking to his master for approval.

"Mm, hmm." The wizard sighed again, stared at the ceiling and whispered, "There's always a woman."

The four gnomes laughed and elbowed one another, saying, "Fuck, fuck, fuck, eh? Haha! Fuck, fuuuuuuck!"

Just then, White, or his most recent incarnation, walked into the cave and smiled at the descriptions his friends were chortling of exactly how they would, serially and simultaneously, violate the beautiful Nios.

He joined in, "Fuck fuck? Ha!"

Zag raised his hands and snapped his fingers. All five gnomes exploded.

When they rejuvenated, Zag said, "Now, listen to me very carefully. I must have that horse in my possession before the joust, now only two days hence. I won't need it for long, only an hour or so, time enough for me to hex the creature and give it back to that caravan of clowns for delivery to King Otto."

Black seemed about to speak. This time, a simple glare from Zag silenced him.

"That means you must capture the horse and bring it to me here tomorrow. I will provide some simple magic to assist you, but it must appear as if you are the thieves, and there must be nothing to trace back to me. Do I make myself clear?"

Afraid to speak, the gnomes merely nodded.

"Good. One last thing. If you fail, I will let you keep your immortal rejuvenation capability..."

The gnomes all smiled, nudging each other.

"... but I will imprison you in this cave, install a wine press, and crush each of you, over and over, for all eternity. I'll then sell the squeezings for hair tonic."

"But" stammered Black, "bald, heads we are, eggs like?"

"Exactly."

Red whispered to White, "Tyl's taint. This guy really *is* an evil fuck."

Chapter 14 - Evil Isn't Going to Cleanse Itself

Not long after Father Sun climbed Mount Tamberlain and leapt into the sky for another day's toil, Oben's troupe prepared to set out for the Second Fork, now with Chanter pulling the cart.

Fil asked Nios to choose which of the two paths they should follow. She walked out to where the road split left and right, stood quietly awhile, then returned and chose left.

Asked why, she said they needed a choice, and with no known reason one was better, either was right.

Fil smiled and said, "Magic ain't just for wizards."

Flap walked ahead, carrying his bow with an arrow nocked. Dongle brought up the rear, turning often to glance down the way they came. Caw rode on Chanter's withers when he wasn't taking quick flights ahead to scout for trouble. Oben now held the reins with Nios smiling by his side. Fil stretched out comfortably in the cart bed, using a soft bag of feed grain as a pillow.

Cautious and alert as the companions were, the way ahead was clear, and the warm morning light lifted their spirits.

Fil watched a herd of puffy white clouds, tinged with the Father's golden brush strokes, migrate lazily across the deep blue morning sky.

"Did you know" he said, "there are some who believe it is Moa who encircles Father Sun, not the other way around?"

"Yes?" Oben said.

"Truly. And wouldn't that be something? The Mother of All, enraptured by her husband's beauty and strength, forever remaining with him when she could, if she wished, fly off to find another husband."

Oben shook his head. "Impossible. The ground under our feet is solid, unmoving. If Moa were flying through the heavens, we'd all be thrown off like chaff from winnowed grain. Nothing could remain where it is, not even Mount Tamberlain."

Flap asked, "From what fevered foreheads do these delusions spring?"

Fil laughed, "From the likes of that feathered fool riding on Chanter's back."

Nios said, "Caw?"

"It's true!" Caw squawked, flapping his wings, "Astrologers and alchemists have been studying for years, and with the gift of flight, I have proven their theories!"

"Proven?" Nios asked.

"Well, proven if I could write down the equations and draw the diagrams. From high above, even higher than Mount Tamberlain, I have achieved viewpoints impossible on the ground. From these observations, I have devised a mathematics demonstrating that Moa is the enchanted one, bedazzled by the light and heat of the Father. It is she who endlessly toils in his service, traveling through the spheres, possessed by his magnificence, in thrall to his attraction. He is the steadfast one, sitting on the throne of the sky, served hand and foot by his beautiful bride."

"It's better that you can't write your formulas and sketch your diagrams" Fil said, "What you claim is heresy, and the priests of Ludd would drag you from the court to the dunking chair to the gallows within an hour if they heard of your so-called proof."

"That's true" Nios said. "The priests wouldn't have it. The Songs of Creation were written long ago by men possessed of Ludd's spirit, and the Songs are quite clear on the topic. Even if you're right, Caw, you'd be condemned."

"Especially if he's right" Fil said. "There's nothing more dangerous than being right at the wrong time."

Nios said, "And anyway, right or wrong, it's bad teaching. What if children learned that it was Moa who toiled for Father, rather than the proper way, the man serving the woman?"

She bumped her shoulder to Oben's and grinned at him. "All would be chaos, the world turned upside down to no good purpose. It's the woman who abides, forming the center of things, holding everything up, the ground from which all life grows. The man toils and gifts all he earns to her so that she may feed and clothe and house her children."

Oben smiled at the lovely woman. "You sound like a priest giving the sermon on First Father Day."

"We've all been in church" she said, "But I like to listen, and I've read and sung the Songs a hundred times. They are a strange and lovely form of poetry, and the stories are what keep us together as a people. Someday, I'd like to sing the Songs to my children." She gazed into Oben's eyes. "To *our* children."

"Bah!" cackled the crow. "Superstition rules the world! It would be worth the trouble to change back into a man, write my thesis and present it to the Royal Academy of Scholars. It's past time we bring down those priests and their ways that keep people stupid!"

Fil laughed, "Just say the word, feather-face. I'll change you back into the two-legged scribbler you were, and speed you to your destiny at the end of the hangman's rope."

Caw flapped his wings in agitation. "No, I'll win this bet first. Then I'll show them just how wrong they are."

"And they'll show you just how superstitious they are. While you're strung up and kicking the air, they'll set you ablaze just to make sure your evil spirit flies back to Mount Fire. I've seen it done. Quite the spectacle."

Caw chattered curses and flapped away to scout ahead.

Oben nodded. "For all their talk of love and brotherhood, the priests are a bloodthirsty lot. I've seen too much violence from them to be a good member of the church. I believe the Songs, but the clergy seem to me just as murderous and greedy as highwaymen."

"Priests bad to Dongle" said the big man. "Hit Dongle lots. Say Dongle no love Ludd. Lie."

Nios looked back. "Oh no, I didn't know that. I'm so sorry, dear, sweet Dongle."

Flap said, "Aye, he was orphaned and held at the monastery near Aflax. Used as a slave, beaten and starved. They had him believing he was bad and shouldn't fight back. But we took care of them, didn't we, old friend?"

"Hehhuhheh, Priest fall long way, go splat. Good fun."

"Yes, indeed. Good fun."

Caw suddenly appeared, screeching and flapping furiously. He landed on Chanter, squawking and pointing a wing down the road.

Fil stood at the noise and watched over Oben's shoulder, listening as the sentient bird clucked and croaked.

He finally found his human voice again and said, "Priests!"

Around the next bend came three priests of Ludd, their long white hair flowing behind them, not covering their naked bums, socks over their cocks, tall white hats gleaming in the sunlight. They carried staffs and small satchels and were chatting quietly as they walked.

Oben pulled Chanter up and stopped the cart.

"Well" Fil said, "speak of evil and here it comes."

"Greetings, siblings" said the first priest as they approached. The tallest, he acted the leader. "How fare you all on this fine day the Father has given us?"

"We are well, Brother Sun" Flap said, tipping his cap and bowing, "And yourselves?"

"We bask in the light of Ludd" intoned the second.

"Blessed are those embraced by Moa and kissed by the Father" said the third.

Nios said, "True words, brother. As we sing in Song Seven" she stood, drew a deep breath and sweetly chanted,

"Moa keeps her children near.
The Father holds the Mother dear.
As always was, the truth is clear,
Ludd's family need never fear."

"Well sung, sister" the leader said, grinning, "and so lovely as well. And yet, as comely as you are, your hair is down. Are you not yet married?"

Winking at Oben, she answered, "Not as such."

The second said, "Perhaps you should join the order, then. You are too great a temptation to the depravities of man to be both unmarried and not cloistered."

"Yes" said the third, eyeing Nios with wicked intent, "Too, too great a temptation."

Oben could see, below the tips of the third's beard, his sock lifting away from his scrawny belly.

The others were likewise becoming turgid.

From the side of her mouth, Nios whispered to Oben, "You've gelded a stallion, haven't you?"

"Yes."

"Care to teach me how?"

Oben stifled a laugh. "Where is your destination this fine day, brothers?"

"Barada" the leader said, "It seems there may be some unholy plot being hatched there, intended to rebel against both crown and church."

"Plot?" Flap said, eyeing Oben and Nios.

"We go to flush out the heretics who threaten the order of things" the second said.

"To cleanse Moa of her wayward children" said the third.

Fil said, "I see. And from what parish do you travel?"

"We are brothers of the monastery at Aflax" the leader answered, standing taller and smiling with pride.

"Aflax?" Fil said, glancing from Flap to Oben to Dongle. "We've heard of the holy order at Aflax."

Dongle's face hardened as he heard the word. A low rumble in his throat sounded like distant thunder.

"I'm not surprised" the leader said, still puffed with self-satisfaction. "We are the most holy of orders, keepers of the sacred Flame of Trope, which washes away the carriers of evil."

"Is that so?" Flap asked, bringing his hand to the nocked arrow.

"Yes" said the leader, "And so, much as we enjoy your company, we can tarry no longer. Evil isn't going to cleanse itself, you know."

"Yes, we know" Fil said, "it must be helped along toward it's day of reckoning."

"Indeed. And so farewell, siblings."

Fil held up a hand. "One thing before you go, brothers?"

"Yes?" said the smiling leader.

He pointed and shouted, "*Amaru eyot showers!*"

Oben gasped, "Where have they gone?"

"Down there, sonny."

Fil jumped out of the wagon and ran to where the priests had stood. He bent and came up holding out his hand.

On his palm wriggled three fat worms.

Everyone gathered around Fil, eyes wide and smiles growing.

He said, "Will anyone speak in defense of the accused?"

Only the breeze spoke in the tallest branches.

"Very well, the court sentences you to death."

He turned his hand over and dropped the worms onto Chanter's back.

Caw let out a screech and gobbled them up with three quick pecks.

Fil dusted his hands. "Evil isn't going to cleanse itself, you know."

Chapter 15 - It's Only Fun if I Catch You

Hours later, the weary travelers found themselves stopped before the Second Fork.

The road veered off in three directions. The left-hand way descended into a ravine, curving out of sight into undergrowth and canopy. To the right, the road took a steep climb toward a nearby ridge. Ahead it continued as it had for some time, flat and straight, with mighty Mount Tamberlain looming in the distance. At the foot of the lofty mountain lay their destination, the gleaming castle of King Otto and Queen Syllabub.

Nios pointed, "Straight on, I'd say. There's the mountain."

"That's the tricky part" Fil said. "When the obvious seems right, you gotta watch your step."

"Oben said, "She was right before. Why not now?"

"I'm not saying she's wrong, sonny. I'm saying we need to be wary of the easy way. The easy way is rarely the right way."

Flap said, "Dear Fil, prince of wizards. Do us a courtesy? Eschew the mysterious and the cryptic falderol and tell us in plain terms which way we should go."

"How about you drop the smart ass schtick, archer, and accept the fact that I'm not sure myself."

"We have to arrive at the castle by tomorrow noon" Oben said.

"Don't rush me, sonny. I'm thinking."

Nios said, "Maybe we should make ready to camp for the night."

Oben shook his head. "We still have light. We should press on."

"Nope" Fil said, "Beauty buns is right. We camp."

Oben objected, "But Fil-"

"Look, can you choose right now? And be sure you will pick the right path? Confident enough" he looked to Nios, "to know your choice will keep your lovely lady here safe?"

Oben turned to Nios, who met his glance with a slight smile but a wrinkled brow, a look that said she would follow him anywhere, even into his missteps.

He looked up the road, left, right, and ahead. "No."

"Right!" Fil smiled and clapped his hands. "So, we camp."

Nios hugged Oben and pecked his cheek. She jumped from the cart saying, "You unharness Chanter. I'll get him some water."

Fil pointed to the right road and said, "Hey, bird brain. Fly up to that ridge and have a look-see."

"Insults and orders at the same time. You really are an asshole, Fil."

"I don't deny it. But this is the only asshole who can put you back in your human skin, so fly away, little birdie."

Caw sighed, "Live ta serve ya, wanker" and flapped his way toward the hilltop.

"Dongle hungry. Go find food." He set off down the hill to the left.

"And me as well" Flap said, following. "With some luck, we'll have rabbit tonight."

As they walked away together, the oaf said, "Dongle like bunny. Pet bunny, no eat."

The archer slapped his huge friend on the shoulder. "Let me tell you about the rabbits, Dongle, in mushroom gravy."

"Hehhuhheh"

Fil walked to a nearby oak tree and sat against the trunk. "I will spend some time in quiet contemplation, seeking insight to our situation."

He settled, laid his hands in his lap and closed his eyes.

Oben said, "You mean you're going to take a nap?"

"A quiet mind is the gateway to understanding."

"Or to sleep" Nios said, grinning.

"The two are not mutually exclusive."

Oben started unbuckling Chanter from the harness, and Nios held the water bucket for him, laughing as the magnificent animal splashed her with his sloppy drinking. Wetted, the silky gown clung to her, and she caught Oben staring at her breasts, nipples dark and hard under the thin fabric. She turned herself to give him a better look.

"When we're married" she said, "Let's have our own horses, and take rides together."

"That sounds nice."

"We could pack a picnic and ride out to Tenshell Grove. Remember?"

Oben remembered. Recalling what they did there, enjoying the sight of her openly teasing him with her barely covered body and wicked smile, rushed blood to his nethers and desire to his heart.

He colored and said, "Yes."

Nios set down the bucket and went to him, embracing his shoulders and pressing herself to his chest. "If the Father and Mother smile on us, that could be where we make our first child. Or..." she slid her hands down, found his haunches and pulled his groin against hers, "... maybe our second."

Oben broke through the overwhelming urge to kiss her and tore himself from her grasp.

As he hurried around Chanter, he said, "We'd better get camp ready. Dongle and Flap could return any time. We'll need to leave tomorrow before dawn, so we should eat and bed down early."

He worked the harness with trembling hands. The smile on her face turned sad.

Oben walked Chanter to a tree and tied him loosely enough to crop grass. Nios took down a crate and a bag from the cart.

Caw returned and lit on a branch in the oak tree. He hopped, saying nothing, moving closer to a spot directly over the wizard's bald head.

"Don't even think it, crack hemp" Fil said.

"What? I didn't want to wake you."

"I wasn't asleep. What did you find?"

"Nothing interesting. After the crest there, the road veers toward Tamberlain, then into a thick wood that doesn't look inviting. Some good rocks for the fire pit are just up by that pine. Nothing else."

"Very well. Fly out over the straight road then."

"You know, I could use a nap myself, and-"

"Begone, beak breath!"

"Tyl's nutsack, old man, grow some manners why don'tcha?"

Caw flapped away, mumbling curses.

Oben started up the hill. "I'll get rocks for the fire" he said as he passed Fil.

"I'd help you, but I've got this bad back, you see."

"Yeah, I see."

Nios brought another load from the wagon near the oak tree. When Oben was far enough away, Fil said, "Don't despair, dear lady. He'll come around."

She watched Oben climb the hill and said, "How can I be sure?"

"You can't. But you can believe you are."

She gave the grizzled little man a puzzled look.

He opened his eyes, grinned, and said, "Think it and it happens."

Her amiable smile returned.

"That's better." He got up, groaning as if every joint were creaking, and dusted off his robe. "Think I'll take a wander up the straight road myself. Got some personal business, too."

"Go careful, Fil."

"Always."

Oben climbed the hill, returned with one large rock, and started up again. He kept to his task and didn't glance at Nios. She did the same, humming one of the Songs.

When Oben was up the hill after the last rock, Nios whispered, "I wonder where Fil is?"

Chanter suddenly neighed loudly and snorted. Nios saw him rear up and kick at the air.

Oben heard the ruckus and turned. Not far down the left road stood a mare, white and blonde as Chanter, signaling her heat. She neighed and whinnied, turning her rump to him and lifting her tail.

Chanter dropped his sheath fast as a drawn sword and shrieked his fury, rearing, kicking and pulling at his lead.

The mare danced again, a full turn with a headshake and neigh, then presented herself, tail high and flared vulva winking.

Inflamed, Chanter suddenly reared against the rope and pulled apart the loose knot at his bridle.

Oben shouted and ran down the hill as Chanter galloped after the mare.

Nios cried out as well, rising just as the great stallion passed her.

The mare bolted down the road and into the forest cover, Chanter close behind, cock flailing and nostrils flaring.

Oben caught up with Nios at the crossroads, helpless as the hoofbeats of the stampeding animals faded in the distance. They stood for a moment, staring.

Oben said, "Where's Fil?"

"He went to scout the straight road."

"We'll never catch them."

"Maybe we can catch up? When they've stopped to couple?"

Oben said, "There's no guarantee they'll end up coupling. It's up to her."

"It is? Hmm. I think I'd like being a mare."

They took a moment from their troubles to pass smiles, one to the other.

Turning back, they shared a gasp. The cart had vanished, and everything on it, save the few things Nios unloaded before.

Oben said, "Thief Gnomes."

Nios said, "That was no mare."

"Zag" they said together and slapped their foreheads.

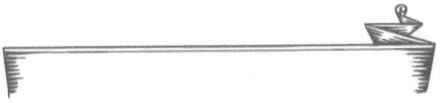

Chapter 16 - Without So Much as a Reach-Around

Outside the cave of the Thief Gnomes, Chanter was in his full glory.

Trapped between a small birch tree and the cave's rock wall, the mare fought to keep her feet as the massive stallion rode her, hooves hammering her back while his long, thick cock pierced deeply with every awkward, insistent thrust.

It would confuse and frighten any passing mortal to hear from the mare the incessant litany of profanity she screamed, in two distinctly humanoid voices.

"Fuck! Fuck!"

"Fuckfuckfuckfuckity fuck!"

Translated, the gnomes Red and Green were begging for release from Zag's spell that condemned them, as the mare's animating force, to endure the painful and humiliating equine shagging.

"Zag! For Ludd's sake man, let us go! Turn the spell! Aaaggghhh!"

"Ogh, ugh, ugh, Zag, make, him, stop!"

Eyes wild, Chanter nipped at the mare's neck, desperate to finish. Soon came a plaintive scream from his throat as he filled her, his semen gushing in great waves and pooling around her legs.

The magician stood nearby, grinning with satisfaction at the plight of the hexed henchmen.

Flap and Dongle also watched but could not react, as they were bound tightly to trees and frozen by Zag's spell. Immobile but conscious, they watched and listened to the piteous begging from the trapped villains, their eyes smiling.

Black, White and Blue also watched from near the stolen cart, grimacing in fear at the thought they might next be the objects of Zag's attention.

Chanter breathed a final snort and fell shaking from the mare's back. He tossed his head and moved unsteadily away, spunk still oozing from his slowly receding sheath.

Zag said, "There's a good boy" and went carefully to the stallion, petting him and cooing as he knotted a lead to the bridle and tied him to the birch.

"Fuck, fuck fuck!"

"I believe" Zag said, still petting Chanter's mane, "that I've made it quite clear I can't understand you unless you speak my language."

"Fuck!" screamed Red.

Green struggled to think, "More no intercourse horse the!"

"More no!" agreed Red.

Zag grinned. No, he's done. More no intercourse horse."

"Fuckityfuckfuck fuck!"

"Try again?"

Blue whispered to his companions, "He really *is* an evil tosser."

Green whined, "Spell please us stop, please!"

"Ah, you said the magic word."

Zag waved a hand and said, "*Cerf rome unhooks!*"

The form of the mare faded. In her place stood the thieves, Green first, then Red, both bent at the waist, Red gripping his brother's belt. They fell over, exhausted.

"Oh, thank Tyl" Green cried in his mother tongue, "that was horrible."

"What are you whining about?" groaned his friend. "I was the one taking that tree trunk up the ass!"

"I had to let him finish" Zag said, strolling toward Chanter's rear and petting his lathered flanks. "He'll be more relaxed and pliant to my magic. You understand, don't you, boys?"

Zag ignored the long string of monosyllables the two wounded gnomes shouted in anger.

"Well, fun time's over" Zag said, dusting his hands, "down to business. It will take some time to prepare, but I want you puny pillocks to be ready to lead the horse back to those dupes as soon as I lay the spell on him."

"Fuck, fuck" Black said, "Mean I, sir, yes."

"You two" Zag pointed to the grumbling half-mares, "go and stoke the fire. I have need to boil a concoction and time is of the essence. Hurry!"

Green and Red scrambled into the cave, mumbling vague epithets in their own language involving the magician, a well-endowed donkey and bear grease.

He pointed to Blue. "You care for the horse. Feed, water, wash him of his seed and brush him out thoroughly."

Blue ran off.

Zag regarded Back and White, tapping his chin with a finger. "I'm beginning to hatch an additional plot that may serve to secure my chances for success. Or at least, provide a pleasant distraction."

They followed him to the cart. He lifted himself into the seat and looked it over, saying, "At first I didn't think this would be useful, seeing as how you little two-legged piranhas ate the jenny."

The gnomes grinned and smacked their lips. Black said, "Best part ears."

Zag ignored their culinary review. "With Fil on their side I'm going to need leverage. And since that dullard Oben is so enamored with his paramour, I know just how to get it."

He turned to Flap and Dongle, helpless. "First, we'll need something to pull the cart."

He raised his arms to the sky, intoning, "*Alpert ... cornily ... woolf*", then pointed his bony hands, one at Flap, the other at Dongle, and shouted, "*defter nooks wyom!*"

Slowly at first, then with more speed, the men transformed. Their bindings disappeared, but the spell still held them. Jerking and shuddering, they fell to their hands and knees. From the tops of their heads sprouted tall, pointed ears as their faces grew long and furry, ending in broad mouths full of huge teeth. Their bodies ballooned in size, ripping through their clothing. Appendages belonging to men faded, replaced by long, skinny legs covered with coarse brown fur, ending in small, black hooves.

After a few more seconds of change, girth increasing, fur growing, tails appearing, the two men completed their transformation into donkeys, one fat and one thin, both braying loudly.

With another wave of the hand, a tall, sturdy fence surrounded them, harsh bits appeared in their mouths, and stout ropes tied them to sturdy posts.

Black and White laughed and applauded the evil wizard.

White said, "Eat! Eat?"

"No, you dim dwarf, you can't eat them. At least not now. Perhaps after they've served their purpose..."

The mere suggestion sent both into fits of gustatory noises and gestures, smacking their lips, rubbing their bellies, pointing to the long ears and saying, "Deep-fried!"

"But meantime, I have another job for the two of you." From a hidden pocket in his robe, he produced parchment and quill. He leaned over the cart bench and began writing.

"Find the archer's bow and quiver" he said.

The gnomes scrambled onto the cart and rifled around. Black found the bow and White the quiver. They immediately began arguing and fighting over the objects.

Still writing, Zag mumbled, "*Ettore goshes*".

A large, heavy iron skillet rose from one box on the cart and dropped heavy blows on one, then the other. They fell to the ground, silent except for whines.

Zag took an arrow from the quiver and tied the letter to it.

"So" he said, "are you two puny putzes ready to get serious about this task?"

"Fuck!" said White, earning him another clanging blow from the flying skillet.

"Yes" whispered Black, closing his eyes and scrunching his shoulders in anticipation.

"Very well. Here is the order you must obey over all others."

He paused, making eye contact with Black, who nodded, then White, still rubbing the lump on his crown.

"She must not be harmed."

Chapter 17 - Bread, Wine, and Blue Balls

Daughter Sun climbed Mount Tamberlain with Warrior Moon following, beginning again the ageless wedding march.

Oben built a small fire. He and Nios sat on logs beside it, silently eating bread she had saved from the cart. As the night grew colder, he covered her shoulders with a blanket. She reached into a wooden crate nearby and lifted out a small wine jug, smiling.

He said, "We're wealthy."

"Beyond compare" she said, uncorking and offering him the jug.

He said, "You first."

"No, husband, you first."

"I am not your husband."

"You are in my heart."

His eyes welled. "And in my heart, you are my wife."

"Then drink, husband. It may be our only chance for a wedding toast."

Taking the wine from her, he raised it and said, "To us."

He drank and passed her the jug.

"To us" she said and drank.

After a moment, Oben collected himself, forced a cheerful tone and said, "So, what other riches did you keep for us?"

"Not much, I'm afraid. But I remembered Song Twenty-Seven and took the bread and wine first."

"I don't remember that song."

She gave him her coy, teasing grin. "You really are a bad Luddian, aren't you?"

"Church bores me."

She laughed, "Twenty-Seven tells the story of Taykin, the first king of Tamberlain, before the city was built. He was chieftain of a small tribe then, and a great fire swept from the grasslands through the forest and finally destroyed their village."

"This sounds familiar" he said, reaching out for the wine.

She handed it to him. "It's best when sung, but the story's good. Some people were foolish and tried to take all their possessions, loading carts and animals with too much to carry, and perished in the flames. Others survived but took their wealth only in metals and stones and fine cloth. But Taykin and his wife, the first queen, Nesta, escaped with only bread and wine."

Oben took another sip and handed her the jug. "She was a baker and he a vintner."

Nios sipped the wine and nodded, "Yes. Other than the clothes on their backs, all they carried away were nine loaves and three casks. The others laughed at him, at first, then cursed him, saying how foolish he was. He told them that bread and wine and his wife was all he needed to live and rebuild."

"I remember this part." Oben cleared his throat and sang brokenly.
"The strength from bread and joy from wine,
Gifts from Father and Moa divine,
Feed the love of man and wife.
These blessings three be the whole of life."

Nios squinted her eyes in a grimace as he finished, "Your singing isn't terrible, but you won't make it into the Chanter's Guild."

He laughed, "All my dreams up in smoke."

"You have other talents."

When he smiled sadly, she said, "You know the rest. Taykin said people could follow him, or not, but he was going to find a better place to live and build a great city. Half went with him while the others went their own way. For months they searched, but Ludd smiled on them, so whenever Taykin and Nesta opened their stores, there was bread and wine enough for all."

Oben said, "And they found the Great River at the foot of the mountain and built Tamberlain."

"Yes."

Oben took the wine from Nios and faced her. He tore a pinch of bread and held it up in his right hand, the jug in his left, the woman framed between.

He said, "These blessings three be the whole of life."

Nios smiled through gathering tears.

"Oben" she said, swallowing the knot in her throat, "my love, please say you will marry me when this is over."

He put the bread in his mouth, washed it down with wine and could not meet her eye.

He said, "This may never be over for us."

"Don't say that."

"If we can't bring Chanter to the king, he'll kill us and maybe others, our families. You heard those priests. There's already rumor of a plot against the king, and suspicion of Barada."

"But we can-"

"Or maybe Zag will kill us. Without Fil, I can't fight him. He may have Fil captive right now, and Flap and Dongle too. Without their help, I can't protect you. All I can do is try to get you home safe, and take the blame for the plot, so the king will leave you and our people in peace. Then you can marry, or fuck every traveler at the inn, I don't care, as long as you can go on living."

Tears flowed and dripped from her chin, but her eyes flashed fury. "I won't let you do that! I'll die with you, or live with you, anywhere, but I won't leave you."

His own eyes burned. "You would put your death on my head? Is that how you would love me? Make me watch you die, at the hands of an evil magician or the jaws of a wild dog? Or the people might hang and burn you in the village square, and to see that as my last image of you ... I couldn't. I can't!"

She wiped her face with her hand and cried, "Would you leave me to pine a lifetime for you, wanting only you, needing only you? Every sunrise, every morsel of bread or sip of wine in my mouth would be a bitter reminder that our love could never be. Every night holding only a pillow instead of you. You would condemn me to that? Is that how *you* would love *me*?"

"Oh, Nios" He bent to hide his face with his hands and drew a deep, shuddering breath.

A quiet cry escaped her throat as she went to him, pulling him up by his hair to plant open-mouthed, hungry kisses on his lips.

He responded, kissing her in return, then fighting against her firm hold.

"Marry me, Oben" she moaned against his mouth, "marry me now, now."

She lifted the hem of her gown, exposing herself, turning to press against him, whispering through tears, "marry me the way that matters, the way of Father and Moa."

"No" he groaned but did not break away.

"Yes, yes, now. Put yourself into me. Put your child into me."

"Oh, Nios, please."

"Yes, please! I'm ready, my body is ready, tonight, this minute. I can feel it, deep inside. Pour yourself into me and I will make us a child, Oben, a child of love, of our genuine love and our proper marriage. Not a pact, an arrangement, but a marriage!"

She squeezed him through his pants and gasped as she felt him respond.

When she tugged at his belt, he pushed her away and stood, groaning and crying, unable to form words. He staggered to the far side of the fire, sobbing into his hands.

"I can't stand saying no to you" he whispered.

"Then don't" she said, breathless.

"A child, now? Without marriage, without your father's consent? Would you burden a child with that? We'd have nothing!"

"We'd have each other."

He wheeled to face her, the face in the firelight wild and frightening.

"We'd be dead in a month! The people of Barada would chase us out with stones and fire. The priests would harry us from village to village. If they didn't catch us and kill us, we'd starve with nowhere to go, nowhere to shelter. Would you watch our child die slowly, painfully, before it ever knew the simple joy of a full belly, a warm bed, a quiet sleep?"

Now she covered her face with her hands and wept.

The forest witnessed their muted sobs in silence.

Nios sat up and wiped her face, then stared into the stars for a moment. He heard her whispering but could not make out her words.

She stood and made for the bushes near the left-hand road.

"Where are you going?"

"Shut up now. I have to pee."

"Don't go far."

"I said, shut up."

He watched until she went behind the undergrowth, then rummaged through their meager stores looking for water.

A faint whistle sang past his ear. A thud drew his eye. The shaft of an arrow quivered against the tree. A ribbon secured a parchment to the shaft, the arrowhead deep in the bark.

He recognized the fletching as Flap's. He pulled it from the tree just as Nios screamed.

The breath he drew to call her name never passed his lips. A flash of pain dropped him into the well of oblivion.

Chapter 18 - Praying Won't Get You Shit

Oben climbed out of the well slowly, in fits and starts, head throbbing with every heartbeat.

From blackness beyond sleep and dreams he stirred, groaned at the tides of pain and fell back. Surfacing again, he smelled dirt and tasted it, gritty in his mouth. The ache and the mulch on his tongue pulled a retch from his throat, sending him again to the depths.

The fire had died to bright coals when he could open his eyes, still on his belly in the dirt and leaves. He saw only dull shapes and flickers of reddish light.

When he could make out the logs by the fire pit, the bread and wine jug on a crate nearby, he spoke his first clear thought silently, *Nios.*

He crawled to the log and sat against it, swished and spat a mouthful of wine before draining the jug.

Eyes closed again, he breathed her name in a sigh, "Nios."

The ache in his head at last eased enough to let the night chill and his thirst reach him. He strained to reach the woodpile and drag a few sticks to the coals. In the crate of provisions he found a skin of water and fought the desire to empty it into his mouth, taking only a few swallows.

His throat wetted, he shouted, "Nios!" and groaned at the pounding ache it rekindled. His word echoed faintly and faded, as if he'd never spoken. He heard the rustling and calls of small creatures cease, spooked by the human cry that spoke their language of loss and need.

From a nearby tree branch, an owl broke the stillness.

Oben heard the rebuke. "Who?" it asked.

Who is here? he thought.

"Who, who?"

No one.

"Who?"

Not even myself.

Still too dazed to fear for Nios or pine for her touch, the thought came to him, *I've never been apart from her.*

He stared into the fire, the new wood crackling, sending sparks into the sky, and stared into the idea in his mind. *Since my birth, not a day has passed without her near.*

The owl asked again, "Who?"

Who am I without her?

"Fool" he groaned, closing his eyes to the ache in his throat.

His mind wandered. He laughed sadly, thinking, *if only I'd paid attention in church, I could pray, and Ludd would help me.*

The sound of her singing came to him, The Songs of Creation in her clear, sweet voice, telling the old stories of Ludd and Tyl, of Father and Moa, of how all things in the world came to be, through love and battle, pain, pleasure, grief and joy.

— *Someday I'd like to sing the Songs to my children.*

"Oh, Nios."

— *To our children.*

Dizzy, he struggled to kneel before the fire, slapped his forehead and bent over his clasped hands.

"Ludd forgive me, Ludd forgive me, Ludd forgive me" he intoned, the first litany to any prayer. He remembered that much at least from his restless, childish time in church.

His vanity fretted. *Why should I debase myself?*

"Fool!" he growled, then rebuked himself in silence, *Will you stand on pride now?*

"Ludd forgive me" he began again, then faltered.

Do I believe in this prayer? Do I believe in Ludd?

Do I believe in anything?

— I'll die with you, or live with you, anywhere, but I won't leave you.

She believes in me.

He sobbed once, the ache flaring, then again, and again.

Remember the Five Pleas, he told himself. *Just start there.*

Eyes closed, the first words from his lips were silent, his lungs empty of the breath to carry them.

Ludd, hear me, a child of Father and Moa calls out.

He drew a shallow breath and spoke.

"Ludd see me, a child of Father and Moa is alone."

He breathed again, struggling to add the simple melody to the words.

"Ludd find me, a child of Father and Moa is lost."

"Ludd lift me, a child of Father and Moa is lame."

For the fifth, the final, his voice loud but wavering with grief, he sang,

"Ludd save me, a child of Father and Moa despairs!"

After a silence, he said, "Not for me, Ludd, my Nios is the lost one, the alone one, the despairing one. I'm not praying for myself, but for her. Help me find her, save her. Give me strength, and guidance, but most of all please, put it in her heart to forgive me. I failed her, I'm to blame, I must make amends. Please, Ludd, through the Father, through Moa, send me the strength to undo what I have done, and I promise-"

A deep voice said, "Praying won't get you shit, you know."

Oben held his breath. In his mind, he said, "Ludd?"

"I take that back" the voice said. "it helps kick your ass into action, but it's not Ludd doing the kicking."

Still not breathing, Oben heard the familiar stamp of a hoof on forest loam, and the lip-flapping burr of a heavy outbreath.

He peeked through narrow lids and saw forelegs, with shiny black hooves. Eyes wide, he gasped at the sight of Chanter, impossibly larger and more rippling with muscle, his coat glistening in the firelight, the thick, flaxen mane flowing to his knee, eyes now half equine and half human with wisdom and compassion.

Oben exhaled, drew a deep, shuddering breath and said, "Chanter?"

He watched with fascination as the large lips and tongue worked to form words.

"Well, my name isn't Chanter, but I do like it. Sort of a nickname."

The man had not yet wondered how the horse came to speak, nor doubted that it would understand him. He said, "What's your name, then?"

Chanter said, "It's a catchy little number that goes like this."

Stretching his neck to the sky, he neighed loud and long, stamped his right front leg three times, snorted, shook his head and let out a deep breath, his fluttering lips resounding, *phlibbhphlibbhh!*.

Oben thought a moment, then said, "Can I just call you Chanter?"

"Yeah. Let's go with that."

"Am I dreaming?"

"No."

"Crazy?"

A familiar voice behind him said, "No more than usual, sonny."

The short, bald wizard made his way into the red glow of the fire.

"Fil?"

"You were expecting maybe a traveling salesman?"

Oben searched for the sense of the moment and found none.

He pointed and said, "Chanter can talk now."

"I talked before. You only half understood me."

Oben turned back the horse and said, "I'm sorry."

"Don't be. I didn't get what you were about half the time myself."

Fil tipped the jug at his mouth, frowned and said, "You drank all the wine, ya greedy bastard?"

"I was thirsty. And my head hurts."

Oben shouted in pain and pulled away from Fil's light touch of his head.

"Whoo boy!" Fil said and whistled, "Yeah, I bet it does. You're gonna need your hat stretched for a while."

Oben tried to stand, shouting, "Nios!", then fell to his knees again and held his palms to his temples.

"Slow down, sonny." Fil led Oben by the arm to sit on the log. "Don't worry, you're gonna get her back, safe and sound."

"I am?"

"Yep."

"How do you know?"

Fil smiled, "Magic ain't just for wizards."

Chapter 19 - Supercilious Wanker, Ain't He?

"Well, look what I found" Fil said. He reached into the provision crate and lifted out a fresh jug of wine.

Oben, beginning to regain his sense, said, "I didn't see that before."

"That's because it wasn't *there* before, sonny."

"What? That's impossible."

Chanter stood cropping grass near the oak tree. He raised his head and snorted, "The man's been talking to a horse, and now he says magic is impossible."

Fil and Chanter both laughed.

From a low branch in the tree, Caw squawked, "Hey, go easy on the poor guy. He's had a hard day."

Fil scoffed. "So look who's suddenly mister nice guy. A crazy alchemist turned into a crow."

"Raven, asshole!"

"That's better."

Fill took a swig of the wine and handed it to Oben. "Here, sonny. You need it more than I do."

Oben sipped from the jug. "We shouldn't sit around here. We need to go after Nios."

Fil sat on a log and threw some sticks into the fire. "Not yet. We've got a lot of work to do. If we're gonna beat Zag, we need to get our magic ducks in a row."

"And you have to *believe* in the magic" Chanter said.

"I'll believe in magic when it saves Nios."

Fil took the wine from Oben. "Naw, that ain't how it works. You gotta believe in the magic first. Then it works, or sometimes it doesn't. But if you start out not believing, then it never works."

"That sounds like a shitty deal."

Fil finished a gulp of the wine and wiped his mouth with his sleeve. "It *is* a shitty deal. Life's a shitty deal. Whatever you try to do, it's at least fifty-fifty you might win, or you might lose. Whatever you don't try, whatever you give up on, one hundred percent guaranteed you lose. So at best, you have a one-in-three chance at anything in this life."

"And still" Caw croaked, "at the end of it all? Boom. Dead."

Chanter said, "Whoa. Cold, dude."

Fil scowled at the bird in the tree. "Thank *you*, sunshine. You're a one-bird pep squad, you know that?

Caw ruffled his wings. "Just being honest."

"Honesty like that we don't need. Now, tell him what you told me about the road."

Caw said, "Right. So, it turns out the road over the hill and through the woods is the fastest, because a couple of miles up the straight road an avalanche cuts it off. If we go right, it bypasses the block and connects again on the far side."

"I checked it myself" Fil said. "The straight road is impassable. That makes the longer route the shortest, because we'd get so far then need to double back here. Remember what I said? The easy way is rarely the right way."

Oben said, "Then let's go. We have to catch up with Zag."

"Just hold your horses, fella", Fil said, then laughed. "Ha! See what I did there?"

Caw screeched, "Ack! Jokes like that we don't need."

Chanter let out a long oboe solo of a fart.

"Sheesh. Everybody's a critic."

Oben stood and shouted, "Dammit! I don't care anymore about taking the horse to Tamberlain! Zag has Nios and I must save her. She's everything to me. Tamberlain and Barada and all of Moa mean nothing if I can't have her. And the three of you sit around here telling jokes?"

Fil's voice suddenly boomed, louder than thunder overhead, "Quiet!"

It echoed from the mountains and scared the forest into silence.

Oben froze, his eyes wide.

Again, the thunder voice. "Sit Down!"

Oben sat.

Smiling, in his normal voice, Fil said, "I'm glad you're all fired up, pissed off, and ready to fight, sonny. We'll need that. Just don't be a fool. Zag has powerful magic. You can't go running at him with a blade and a scream. He'll burn you to ashes and then everybody dies, including Nios. So, cool your balls and work with us here. We'll save Nios, and maybe the whole of Tamberlain and Aflax while we're at it."

Caw flapped his way down and landed on Chanter's back. "Quite the motivational speaker."

Chanter nodded his enormous head. "Yeah, like a slave army captain."

Fil stared at Oben, waiting.

Oben sighed, swigged the wine and said, "Okay."

"Good, now we're getting somewhere. So, like I say, we can leave at first light and make it to Tamberlain in time by riding Chanter, here. Especially now that he's enchanted, because-"

The horse snorted. "Uh, hold up, gramps. That's going to be a problem."

Oben said, "Why?"

"Because Zag didn't throw his spell on me to make me talk, even if I do have a beautiful speaking voice and perfect diction."

"What's the deal, then?" Fil asked.

"Anyone who rides me, dies."

Caw screeched and flew to the highest branch.

"At anything past a walk, I mean."

Oben frowned. "I don't understand."

The horse lip-fluttered an outbreath. "I'll be King Otto's steed in the joust."

Fil said, "Yeah?"

"So he mounts, walks me to the lists, and all's well. He spurs me to charge, he drops dead. That's the spell."

"Ludd's beard" Oben whispered.

Fil's eyes widened. "Hod wins the joust, and Tamberlain."

Oben finished the thought. "And Zag is Vizier to a kingdom twice as big."

Chanter shook his head. "It's worse than that. By tradition, the winner of the king's joust mounts his enemy's horse and takes a victory lap around the arena. At a gallop."

"Hod dies" Fil said, "and there is no king."

Oben said, "What about Queen Syllabub?"

"She's queen consort. She can't take the throne. And they are childless."

Oben spoke slowly. "Zag will declare himself ruler."

This time, Fil finished Oben's thought. "Of all Tamberlain and Aflax."

"Tyl's demons" croaked Caw, "He really *is* an evil fuck!"

Oben stared into the fire, then said to Chanter, "But why did he give you the ability to tell us all this?"

"He didn't" Chanter said with a shake of his mane. "Giving me speech was a mistake. I don't know how it happened, but me revealing his plan was not part of the plan."

"At least he's a fuck up of an evil fuck" Caw said.

Fil stood and began pacing. "We still have the problem of getting to the king in time. If we can't ride Chanter, we'll never make it."

Oben said, "What if we start now?"

"Not even then. And believe me, sonny, there are things in the woods ahead you don't want to face at night."

Oben dropped his head and sighed.

As he paced, Fil stared, unfocused, at the ground. Something caught his eye. He bent and came up with the arrow.

"What's this?"

Oben stood and hurried to Fil's side. "That was fired at me just as they took Nios. I'd forgotten."

Fil untied the parchment and scrolled it open. He read,

"*Hear the command of the invincible Grand Vizier Zag, and obey, on pain of death.*"

"Supercilious wanker, ain't he?" said Caw.

"*You will deliver the horse to King Otto at noon tomorrow and assist with his mounting for the joust. Do not ride the steed, or you will surely die. If you fail, or if you speak my name, I will kill your woman slowly, painfully, and repeatedly, reviving her only to die again a thousand times.*"

Oben stared into the fire, drawn lips and burning eyes a mask of rage.

Fil began to laugh and cavort, waving the parchment and shouting, "This is it! I have it!"

Oben glared at the little wizard. "What are you doing dancing and giggling at a time like this? I'll-"

"No, sonny, no! Listen, this is how we defeat him."

"How?"

"With his own magic."

Fil re-rolled and tied the letter around the shaft.

"We have this!" He lifted and pointed the arrow to the sky.

"One arrow?"

"Strike the right target, and a single arrow can win a war."

Chapter 20 - The Part Where the Villain Gloats

The fire in the cave of the Thief Gnomes crackled and roared, freshly stoked with dry softwood.

On one side stood the thieves, gazing with rageful lust at Nios on the other, tied to a stake. Her thin gown was now tattered, exposing her deep cleavage and one firm, white thigh to her shapely hip. The struggle against capture had taken a toll on her strength. She heaved to regain her breath, her long black hair disheveled and hanging in her eyes.

The attackers bore the brunt of the casualties. She killed two with her flashing dagger, slitting one's throat and stabbing the other directly in the heart. When they reappeared, she changed tactics and dealt only wounding cuts and blows. Now, Red and Blue were bleeding from slashes to arms and legs, and Green had lost a finger. Nios had rained savage pommel strikes on White's face, leaving him bruised and nearly toothless. Black stood bent slightly, cradling his crushed testicles in his tiny hands.

Only with a coordinated assault could they bring her down, like wolves on a mother bear.

Nursing wounds and groaning in pain, they muttered their lewd observations and prurient plans for her, sounding to Nios like a flock of woodpeckers given the power of speech and cursing with every head-pounding peck.

Her eyes showed neither fear nor anger. She looked on the tiny men with a grin of patient disdain, like a mother catching her pubescent boys in a circle jerk.

"You really are a passel of pathetic wankers, aren't you?"

The rapid-fire string of *fucks* increased in speed, volume and pitch as the gnomes grabbed their crotches, thrust their hips, wagged their tongues and mimed fondling her breasts. One pointed to her, then pretended to hold a cock and shove it in his mouth.

"Just you try it, squirrel dick" she sneered. "I'll bite it off and have it for lunch."

The agitated goblins seemed ready to make good on their threats when a sudden flash of light outside the cave entrance and a ground-shaking clap of thunder made the gnomes scream and huddle together against the far wall like a litter of frightened puppies.

Grand Vizier Zag stepped through the entrance, stiff-backed and haughty. He stood regarding Nios in the firelight.

Not taking his eyes from her, he hissed, "I believe I made it abundantly clear that the woman was not to be harmed."

Just as the litany of desperate monosyllables reached a crescendo, Zag held out his left palm and hammered it with his right fist.

Like five mice under a war mallet, the gnomes flattened and splattered to a sickening chorus of crunching bones and squishing flesh.

A few seconds later, they reappeared at the opposite wall, dazed and staggering.

Before they could start their chattering again, the magician pointed at them and chanted, "*Cutup heft husk!*"

The tiny thieves posed frozen as they stood immobile and silent.

Zag again faced Nios and gave her a shrugging smile. "I do apologize sincerely for the incompetence of my staff. They were under strict orders to bring you here without mussing a single eyelash on your beautiful face."

Nios smiled. "Please, don't give it a second thought. If you'll just spot me a few coins for a new gown, I'll be on my way and no harm done."

"I'm afraid I can grant only one of your requests."

Zag waved his hands at Nios, from head to toe, and muttered, "*Emory shorts toxify.*"

The shredded, bloodstained white dress faded. In a heartbeat, Nios wore a shimmering, body-hugging gown of silk in blood-red, flowing from a plunging neckline to follow every curve and gather at her feet. Her onyx-black hair was coiffed, drawn at the temples and cascading down her back in thick, shining ringlets.

"I hope you don't mind" Zag said. "They say a winter palette like yours calls for greens or blues, but I like to buck the trends, don't you?"

"It's truly lovely, thanks. Don't bother wrapping it, I'll wear it home."

"Yes, about that. When you go home, or *if* you go home, is a question that can only be answered tomorrow noon and depends entirely on how your friend Oben carries out my orders."

"He's not my friend. He's my husband."

"I stand corrected. If your husband wishes to save you, he has only to follow my instructions without fail. Do you believe he will do that?"

"Oben will do what's right."

"Right for you?"

Nios hesitated only an eye-blink, then raised her chin. "He'll do everything he can to save me. But in the end, he will make a hero's choice, no matter what."

"A hero's choice" Zag repeated.

He paced slowly around the fire and tapped his chin with a long, bony finger. "That's an interesting phrase. It assumes the hero has a clear vision of what is the right thing to do, even when the challenge he faces is very complicated, with effects far beyond his understanding."

Nios hesitated, then grinned. "Is this the part where you gloat and reveal your plot?"

Zag stopped pacing and met her eye. "What?"

"Mine isn't the best father in the world, but when I was a girl he read bedtime stories to me every night. In those stories, whenever some evil shit like you was just about to spring his trap, he'd suddenly start running off at the mouth, ego showing like a wedding dick and absolutely aching to tell somebody what a genius he is."

Zag started to speak, but she cut him off.

"So the idiot goes blathering his head off to someone, anyone, because he just can't stand to not get the credit he's due. Sometimes it's the girl he's captured, hint-hint, or he'll talk the ear off the hero he's about to kill, and he reveals his plans, or lets slip some clue to his weakness. Is that this part, now?"

Zag recovered himself and bellowed, "This is not a story!"

"Everything is a story, mister genius. Stories make the world. This is our story, and we've come to the part where you get your say. Tell me, then, oh great and powerful Zag, about the trap you've set for my Oben, my hero."

Zag stared at the woman in red, a finger held against his sunken cheek. "The trap is not for your hero. It is for kings Otto and Hod. Oben and that horse are the spring and hammer of the trap. If he fails me I will kill him, you, and every living thing in Barada down to the fleas on your dogs. If he follows my orders, and succeeds, I will be king, no, I will be *emperor* of all the land. I will raise him up in my court, and you with him."

Zag smiled faintly, his arms crossed. "What do you think of that hero's choice, beautiful storyteller?"

Nios smiled back. "I think I know exactly what Oben will do. So sure that I propose a wager."

Zag's thin eyebrows arched. "Yes? I'm listening."

"If you become emperor, you will be in need of an empress, will you not?"

Zag's smile grew. He nodded, saying nothing.

Nios shifted her weight, bending one knee to throw the other hip out in sharp relief. She leaned forward, her hands trapped behind her, making her breasts sway against the deep neckline of the gown. Dipping her chin, she held Zag's eyes with her own, soft and glistening under heavy lids.

"If Oben obeys you, then he is no husband to me, and my world will end. If he does that, I will be your consort. You will have me, body and soul, for I will no longer belong to him, or to myself."

She could see her magic work on the dark man. Eyes wide, pupils dilated, his breath came fast but weak, and his sallow cheeks flushed.

"You are that sure of him?"

She nodded and smiled. "I believe in our story."

"So, you believe he will fail me. What then?"

Her smile brightened. "In that case, you will die, and I will have the man I love for all my remaining days. Oh, and I'll piss on your grave."

The vizier nodded. "You drive a hard bargain."

"One more thing."

"Yes?"

"If he obeys you, and makes you emperor, you must kill him, swiftly and without pain. Otherwise, you'll have to kill us both."

Zag's face lost its blush. Gaping, he said, "Why?"

"Because I could never live down the soul-killing shame of his eyes on me when I am consort to a disgusting, parasitic slug like you."

The smile returned tenfold, his forehead forming chevrons of evil joy.

"You, lovely Nios, have a very big mean streak. I accept."

Chapter 21 - Again With the Thigh Wound

Oben woke to the sound of boiling liquid and an acrid, nose-burning smell.

He pulled his head from under the blanket and blinked to clear his sight. Morning twilight faintly illumined the crest of Mount Tamberlain, as The Father was just beginning to stir from his bed.

Outlined in the firelight, Fil sat hunched over a small cauldron of whatever foul brew assaulted Oben's nose, stirring and mumbling incantations.

Chanter stood dozing by the oak tree, the breath from his great nostrils puffing clouds of steam in the pale light. Perched on his withers sat Caw, beak drooped, and eyes closed, murmuring in his sleep. Oben heard familiar words like *science* and *swallows*, but the rest, talk of *airspeed velocity* and *weight ratios*, came from a height of learning beyond his ken.

He sat up and was about to speak when Fil said, "Nope. Don't say a word, sonny. I've been working on this all night. You bump my elbow now and I ruin the whole batch. So just... don't"

Oben stood and stretched, drank from the waterskin and splashed some on his face. He heard Chanter stir and snort, startling Caw awake.

"A duck!" the bird screeched, flapping his wings wildly.

Oben went to them, shushing, his finger at his lips.

"Be quiet. Fil's working on some kind of potion."

Caw shook his head. "Phew. Rank. I thought it was Chanter's piss."

126

On cue, Chanter let go with a long, heavy emission, splashing into a widening puddle in the dirt at his feet.

Caw squawked and flapped away, choking. "Awk, That's worse!"

"Perfect timing" Fil said. He used a piece of leather to take the cauldron by its handle, then waddled to Chanter and held the pot directly under the horse's stream. The mixture hissed and fumed, making Oben cough and Chanter whinny as they both backed away.

"Just right" Fil said, waddling back to the fire. "Almost ready."

He went back to stirring the brew and muttering.

Chanter and Oben kept their distance from the fire, the horse saying, "You think he knows what he's doing?"

"One way or the other, he's our only hope."

Caw found his way back and lighted on Chanter. "I hate to give the asshole credit, but he's the best, or near as dammit. If he says he's got a way to pull our nads out of the fire, the only thing that'll stop him is bigger magic."

"Like Zag's?" Chanter said.

"Yeah, like Zag's."

"Zag's magic ain't fly shit" Fil said. "He's got only one thing over me."

Caw squawked, "Fashion sense?"

"Zero conscience. Without one, you can do anything."

"You taught me if I think it," Oben said, "it can happen."

"Exactly, sonny. Now imagine someone with that power who would happily burn down the whole world to get what he wants."

Fil took the pot off the fire and set it on the ground. "Now, we let that cool a little, then we find out if you live or die."

Oben looked to Chanter, then to Caw. "If *who* lives or dies?"

"You, sonny. You're the one has to ride the horse to get us to Tamberlain in time."

Oben looked to the west where the Father had just stepped from his door at the foot of the mountain to begin the long climb to his workday.

Fil stirred the cooling mixture, making quiet noises that sounded half like words and half like the warbles and squeals forest creatures speak when no human can hear.

Oben pointed to the little cauldron. "So, how does it work?"

Fil laughed. "It works by working. If I could explain how it works, it wouldn't work."

"Okay, then, what do I do?"

"Ah" Fil smiled and wagged a finger, "*that's* the question to ask. It's the doing that matters."

"All right, then. Tell me."

Fil winked and waved a hand. "Come over here, sonny."

He led Oben past the shadows of the forest into a clearing where they could see Mount Tamberlain to the west and the smoking crest of Mount Fire in the east.

"The first thing you have to do is three things. I have only a few minutes to teach you, more's the pity. It usually takes a lifetime."

"Then how can I learn them now?"

"You want Nios back?"

"More than anything."

"That's how."

Oben looked west, felt the heat of the sunlight on his face, then east, and felt the Father place a warm and loving arm around his shoulder.

"Okay."

"First" Fil said, holding up a stubby finger, "be brave. That doesn't mean you don't have fears. It means you go forward anyway, no matter how scared you are."

"Be brave" Oben repeated.

"Next, be calm. All fear is fear of death, and you're going to die anyway, so it might as well be today. Tell fear to fuck off."

Oben nodded. "Be calm."

"Finally, be sure. Whatever you do, do it without second thought. Don't think this or that, just do, just act. Falter, and you fail."

Oben closed his eyes. "Be sure."

"There you go, sonny" Fil said, slapping Oben's back and smiling. "Fifty- or sixty-years' worth of training in five minutes. Can't beat it at twice the price."

Oben returned the smile. "What now?"

"Now, you live or die."

Fil walked back to where he had left the cauldron of foul potion and gave it a last stir. He took a small empty bottle from the crate, ladled some of the liquid in, corked it and shook it. Then he took up Flap's arrow with Zag's letter tied fast and handed both to Oben.

"The arrow is the help of your friends to increase your strength. The letter is your enemy's weakness to use against him. The potion is Moa, your mother's blood, to sustain your life."

Oben looked from the arrow to the bottle, his brow furrowed.

Fil said, "Dip the arrowhead in the potion."

Oben uncorked the bottle, slid the tip of the arrow in and removed it. The razor-sharp iron blade glowed red, as if heated in a forge.

"The rest is very simple" Fil led Oben to Chanter. "Mount him, spur him to a trot, and before you die stab him and yourself with the arrow."

Oben gasped, staring at Fil.

Caw laughed and cackled. "Ain't that just like the dried up old skinbag? Hey kid, it's simple, just don't die! Haw haw!"

Fil gritted his teeth. "Shut yer beak, feather dick."

"Haw! You should add *be stupid* to your life lessons, ya rotten old fake!"

Fil pointed at Caw and shouted, "*Abba Egon stithy!*"

Caw vanished.

Oben gasped. "Where'd he go?"

"He's fine, the little putz" Fil said. "I sent him about ten miles away. By the time he gets back, we'll know."

"We'll know what?"

Fil shrugged.

"Oh."

Oben handed the bottle to Fil and went to Chanter.

"Are you okay with this?"

The horse snorted. "I'm not wild about the arrow thing."

"Just a little jab" Fil said, "enough to get a tiny bit of potion into you both. Too much, and I have no idea what might happen."

Chanter eyed Oben. "Very reassuring" he said.

Oben asked Fil, "This won't hurt him, will it?"

"It'll sting a bit."

"But I die, not him?"

"Only you, sonny."

Oben patted the horse's neck. "Chanter?"

"You only die once. Hop on."

Oben clamped the arrow's shaft in his teeth and vaulted onto Chanter's back. Gripping a handful of mane with his left hand, he took the arrow in his right and urged Chanter into a slow walk.

They circled the small clearing once. Oben squeezed with his legs to urge a trot. His vision blurred, so he hurried to poke Chanter's rump with the arrow, enough to spur an "Ouch" and draw a trickle of blood.

Oben then jabbed his own right thigh with the arrow and died.

Chapter 22 - I Was Dead but I'm Better Now

In windless free fall, Oben passed through untold gossamer threads alight with lives embodied in breath and bone and sparkling spirits in myriad colors defying name.

Through never-passing-never-ending time, over uncharted landless lands, under deep waterless seas Oben flew, his eyes glimpsing all faces, ears hearing all songs, tongue speaking all words, flesh tingling with the embrace of all arms, moving without motion from then to now from there to here from one to all.

A point of light appeared, a pinprick in the fabric of space growing larger, until it surrounded him in a universe of nothing but light.

"You're early" a soundless voice said.

"Early?" he said without speaking, "for what?"

"For this. For here."

"I like it here."

"Of course, you do. It's easy."

"Easy?"

"No work. No trouble. No pain."

"Yeah" Oben said, smiling, "It feels good."

"Sure it does, but that's all it does."

"Can I stay?"

"Sorry. You're early."

Oben began to recognize the voice.

"Are you teasing me?"

Oben heard the smile in the answer, "No, I would *never* do that."

"You're teasing me. I can stay if I want."

"Yes, that's true, you can stay if you want."

"Then I'll stay."

"Aren't you forgetting something?"

"Am I?"

"Before you came here. You were doing something."

Oben hesitated, "I was?"

"Yes. Can you remember?"

Oben thought. He couldn't recall anything prior to the light and the voice.

The voice said, "You were doing something important."

"It's hard" he said. "I can't seem to remember."

"Try. It was important. To you."

"To me? Who is me?"

"The me that is you right now before you came here. That's your me, the me who was doing something important to them, then."

Oben laughed silently. "That's not the me now, though."

"Yes, and no" the voice said, "you're still that me even now as long as you don't stay here. But if you stay, then that me won't be you anymore and you will not do what the me who came here believed was very important to do, there and then."

"Wow" Oben said, "when I got here it was easy. Now it's hard."

"Yes, it is difficult. It gets worse. If you stay, then you'll remember the me that is you now and you'll remember what you were going to do that was so important and you will know that you didn't do that important thing and you will quite probably regret not having done it."

"Now I know you're teasing me."

Like the smile before, Oben heard the sad eyes in the voice. "No. I wish I was."

Oben tried again. "I don't know. It's like there was nothing before."

"Oh, there was something. There was something so much better than what is here."

"Better? That sounds impossible. It's so nice here."

"Yes. That's the problem."

Oben struggled again and failed, though he couldn't think at what.

The voice said, "What is the last thing you remember, before coming here?"

Oben felt something and said, "I hurt my thigh."

"How?"

Again he struggled. "I... I stabbed myself."

"Why?"

"I don't know."

After a moment, the voice said, "What did you use to stab your thigh?"

It came to him. "An arrow."

"Why would you stab yourself in the thigh with an arrow?"

"Sounds crazy, doesn't it?"

"It sounds important."

Oben struggled again. The ease he felt in the light faltered.

"I think" he said, his words coming slowly, "I was riding a horse."

"So, you were riding a horse and you stabbed yourself in the thigh with an arrow?"

"Yes."

Oben felt a tug at his mind and heart, a force pulling him away from the light. He saw his hand gripping a horse's mane, heard the hoofbeats of the horse running, felt the sharp pain in his thigh.

"I needed to ride the horse somewhere."

"Yes?" the voice said, and Oben heard the smile return. "Where?"

The pull strengthened. He felt the rhythm of the magnificent animal running beneath him, the ache in his legs as he gripped to keep his seat. He heard the horse's breathing, deep and loud.

"To Tamberlain."

"Where is Tamberlain?"

"It's... back there."

"Back where you're the me who was doing something important?"

"Yes."

"What is in Tamberlain?"

"I don't know."

"*Who* is in Tamberlain?"

Oben felt impatience grow inside his chest like a fire, the pull now harder on his heart and the pleasant glow of the light fading.

"Why can't you just tell me?"

"Because that's not how it works."

"Are you Ludd?"

The voice laughed, and Oben heard the laugh he'd heard all his life.

"No" the voice said, "I am not Ludd."

"Nios!"

"Oben!" Fil shouted. "Hey, sonny, you okay?"

Oben found himself atop Chanter, gripping his silky mane in his left hand as the majestic animal trotted a circle in the forest clearing. In his right hand, he held the arrow. He noticed the sharp pain in his thigh and saw a bloodstain on his trouser leg.

"Hold up, sonny! Whoa!"

Oben leaned back to signal Chanter to walk, then stop.

Fil ran to his side. "You all right?"

"Yes" Oben said as the tingle in his sinews faded away. "I think so."

"Then it worked! Whoo hoo!" Fil started dancing, waving his arms and singing, "You didn't die, you didn't die, you-"

"I think I did."

Fil stopped dancing. "Did what?"

"Die."

"Well, you're looking pretty good for a dead guy."

"I wanted to stay."

"Dead?"

"Yes."

"Why?"

"It was so nice, pleasant, easy."

"Why'd you come back?"

"Nios."

"Right" Fil said and slapped his bleeding thigh.

"Ow! What was that for?"

"To remind you what you're doing and who you're doing it for, sonny. Remember, the easy way is rarely the right way."

Oben dismounted and stroked Chanter's muscular neck.

"How are you, boy?"

"Fine. That little stick in the rump wasn't too bad. And I was enjoying the run."

Fil said, "You're gonna get a chance for a nice long run, beauty boy. This means we can get to Tamberlain in time."

Oben said, "Okay, what now?"

"First, I need a bit of help. Give me the arrow."

Fil took the arrow, dipped it in the potion and jabbed his thigh.

Oben watched as the small man stiffened, his face blank, then recovered.

"Wow" Fil said. "Now I get why you wanted to stay."

"Nice, wasn't it?"

"Too nice. Glad someone was there to school me, or I'd be there now."

Oben said, "We have to hurry."

Fil shook his head and shivered. "Right." He found a satchel among their provisions and started filling it with the waterskin, bread, and the vial of potion.

He handed the bag to Oben. "Keep this and that arrow handy. It's big magic, and we're gonna need it."

Oben kicked dirt over the last of the campfire coals. "What do we do when we get there?"

"We'll have to figure that out as we go, sonny. Just remember what I said about the three things."

Oben tied the arrow to the satchel and threw it over his shoulder. "Be brave, be calm, be sure." He climbed atop Chanter and helped Fil up to sit behind him.

"And if all else fails" Fil said, "be crazy. It'll confuse 'em long enough to give you an opening."

"Crazy like you?"

"No, like you, a man in love. There's nothing crazier."

Oben said, "Hang on!" and urged Chanter forward at a full gallop up the high road and over the ridge, racing toward the glittering capital city of Tamberlain.

Chapter 23 - Get On With It

Helmets and shields flashed in the bright midmorning sun as rival knights fought in the lists of Tamberlain. The castle's soaring spires of gleaming pink sandstone stood watch over the field of honor.

Heavy horses in heraldic caparison thundered across the sand and sawdust of the arena, their riders shattering lances and shields, the crowd leaping to their feet and cheering each bone-crushing clash.

The fighters prepared for battle in striped tents ringing three sides of the field, with horses tied nearby and weapons displayed, flags of family crests undulating slowly in the gentle breeze. On the fourth side, troupes of musicians and acrobats in brightly colored costumes gamboled before the tall wooden stands in hopes the spectators might toss them a coin or an apple or a crust of bread.

Knights awaiting a contest paraded before the seats with squires in tow, preening for the attention of the ladies in the upper decks. As they passed, they bowed before the gabled dais where King Otto, his Queen Syllabub and King Hod of Aflax sat side-by side in ornate chairs of rich wood and tapestry cushions.

Otto, rounded by indolence and rich food, sweated in his heavy white tunic and silver breastplate, despite his youth. He had already drunk more wine than was wise, given his turn in mere hours to face his own challenge. Meeting Hod in the lists at midday would make him king of two lands or just another dead monarch, ridiculed by history for his failure until forgotten and unsung after generations passed.

To his left sat gracious Queen Syllabub, blond, tall, and full-breasted, her long gown of gossamer pink fabric stressing every curve and line. She leaned to her left often, giving Hod glimpses of her smooth white cleavage flushed peach with excitement. She kept her eyes on the dark, bearded man in all black clothes and breastplate, asking him questions about his home in Aflax, not seeming to mind that he never answered.

Hod did not ignore the blushing woman. He watched her out the corner of his eye, sometimes smiling and nodding at her awkward flirting, biding his time, knowing she would soon be his to use as he wished. Not long after this day, he swore to himself, she would grow round-wombed with his first heir and he would breed her each time she came to season, fathering a dynasty that would grow in the fullness of time to rule all of Moa.

A hissing noise rose in volume from the far side of the grandstand. First only a few voices, then a dozen, then scores of people sibilated their displeasure. The sound approached the royals like waves of an incoming tide.

Otto said, "Ah, Zag must be on his way."

The tall, gaunt vizier strode through the crowd, ignoring their catcalls and muttered curses. Head high, he reached the kings and queen and bowed deeply, his smile tinged with the anticipation of triumph.

"My lord and liege" he intoned as he stood, "your magnificent majesty King Otto, sovereign of Tamberlain and the unincorporated areas south-west of the mighty river Krunt, patron of the arts and sciences, beloved of the people."

Otto drained his wine cup, belched and said, "Yep, that's me."

Bowing again Zag said, "Lovely, gracious Syllabub, delicate flower of Tamberlain, lady of hearts, from whose strong thighs shall soon issue forth a line of succession to last a thousand years, consort to Otto, and queen of all the land."

The queen yawned and threw Zag a two-fingered salute accompanied by a long, loud raspberry.

With only a nod of his head, Zag addressed the rival king. "Your highness, ruler of Aflax, defeater of The Really Bad-Tempered Boar of the North, Hod the Quiet, Hod the Strong, Hod the Not-To-Be-Trifled With, we welcome you to the field of battle this fine day."

"Get on with it" Hod said, sneering.

"Indeed" Otto said, "get on with it. Where is my gift, Zag? The horse from the people of Barada?"

"I am confident, sire, that it will arrive soon. A young man named Oben, the brilliant horseman and blacksmith who trained your magnificent beast, is bringing him directly, I'm told. Magistrate Gustall assured me of this man's probity and bravery in traversing Fuckall over the Forked Road to speed the animal here today."

Otto leaned to his guest and said, "Nice of my people to offer me such a fine gift, eh Hod? My people love me because I love them. I doubt anyone in Aflax ever sends you gifts, do they, you rotten old fart sack?"

"I don't need to be given anything, you fat swamp rat." Hod eyed Syllabub and said, "I take what I want."

The queen smiled and flushed, eyeing the glowering king and running a finger delicately from the hollow of her throat to the drop of perspiration between her breasts.

"You'll take my lance up your ass at midday, you bearded pile of dog shit."

"I'll take your skull back to Aflax and use it to eat soup, you drunken cat fucker."

Zag held up his hands, pleading, "Gentlemen, sires, sovereigns. I beg you save your venom and vigor for the field of honor. This contest will bring to conclusion all your past rancor and feuding, but for now, let us enjoy the tournament, some refreshment, and bask in the beauty of our gracious queen."

Zag bowed again, offering Syllabub an oily smile.

"Bite me, maggot," said the queen.

Otto's face went pale as he motioned to Zag for a conference. The magician leaned close.

"You're certain the horse will guarantee me victory?"

"That is what Magistrate Gustall assured me, sire. He spoke of the amazing skills this Oben has for training horses. The majestic steed Thunderhooves will nip at Hod's horse at the crucial moment, spooking his mount just as you thrust your lance home to his heart."

"Excellent, Zag. My eternal gratitude to you for finding this Thunderhooves and the people who offer him to their king. I shall reward you and them handsomely."

As he stood, Zag again greased his smile and said, "Your virtue, sire, is exceeded only by your generosity."

"Do you hear, darling?" Otto said, nudging the queen's arm, "the steed is named Thunderhooves."

The queen yawned. "Of *course* he is."

Otto's mouth grinned, but his eyes grimaced as he signaled to a page for more wine.

Zag said, "With permission, I shall take my leave and inquire as to the horse, your majesty."

The queen glared and said, "Don't stand on ceremony, shitbird. You always have permission to go."

"Yes, of course, a thousand thanks, beloved queen."

As Zag bowed and walked away, Hod stood and said, "Well, I've got to, uh, drain the snake. Be right back."

"Do you need help?" Syllabub said, leaning toward Hod.

"Help?"

"A hand, or... something?"

Hod caught her meaning and allowed himself to grin. "Perhaps, your highness, on another occasion."

The dark king enjoyed his thoughts of the woman's heaving bosom and dilated eyes as he hurried to find Zag.

He spotted the magician under the grandstands and took hold of his arm, pulling to force Zag to face him.

"What were you saying to Otto just now?" Hod said, scowling.

Zag silently glanced at the grip on his arm and then met the king's eye.

Hod's face lost color, and his breathing became labored. He shook his head and released Zag's arm.

Zag held Hod's gaze and said, "I was assuring him of his victory, as any vizier would do for his king. Would you have me do otherwise?"

Hod looked away, shaken, and said, "No, of course not. I just... wonder at your loyalty to me."

"And by my continuing subterfuge, Otto will not question my loyalty to him. Thus our plan has the best chance at succeeding, does it not?"

Collecting himself, Hod said, "Yes, it does. And you are sure his horse will bring me victory?"

"I am told the steed's training is thus, that he will shy away just at the crucial moment of the joust, throwing Otto's aim off and allowing you to run him through like a pig on a spit. Victory for you is certain, as is my position as Prince of Tamberlain, and ruler of these lands, yes?"

"Yes, magician" Hod said, finally gathering his confidence, "win Tamberlain for me, and I will let you rule it and squeeze the land and the people for every coin, every drop of blood, and every loaf of bread, in my name and to my benefit."

"Then we understand each other. Unless you have other concerns you wish to voice?"

Again Hod steeled himself. "No, Zag. We understand each other."

"Excellent. Now if you will excuse me, I must go to ensure success of the plan that I, Grand Vizier Zag, have crafted to make you, Hod of Aflax, sovereign of Tamberlain."

Hod stood, saying nothing.

"With your permission" Zag said, bowing only with his eyes. He said no more and walked into the crowd.

Out of Hod's earshot, Zag grinned evilly and muttered, "Sovereign of Tamberlain for a few heartbeats, that is."

Chapter 24 - We Wants the Redhead

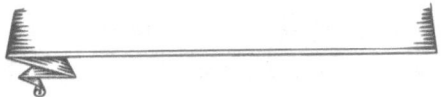

For miles Chanter galloped without pause, ears flat and tail flying like a flag, the chugging breath of his great lungs as loud as the rumble of his hooves on the path.

Oben sat him as if joined, leaning low to his massive neck, gripping the mane as he matched the sway of his body to the animal's pounding gait.

Fil held tight to Oben's tunic and tried to blend with animal and man despite his short legs flailing, while Caw flew just steps behind, flapping his shiny black wings as fast as he could to keep pace.

Oben noticed a change in Chanter's breath and said, "Whoa, boy, let's find water."

The horse kept running and puffed words between deep breaths, "I. Can. Still. Go."

"No, you need rest, hold up."

"But-"

Oben leaned back, nearly throwing Fil off, and the stallion obeyed, slowing to canter, trot, and finally walk, snorting and tossing his head. Caw lighted on Oben's shoulder, and for a time the companions moved slowly along the Forked Road, catching their breath.

Once quieted, Oben heard the burbling of a small creek in a gully. He shifted his body to turn Chanter off the road. In a few more steps, they reached the stream. Oben dismounted and helped Fil down as Chanter bent his head to drink. Caw flapped his way into a small, eddied pool and drank, then ducked and fluttered in the water.

Oben said, "Slow, boy."

Chanter only snorted and kept lapping at the cold, crisp water.

Fil took a few unsteady steps, rubbing his flanks and stretching his back. "Whoo boy, I ain't gonna sit for a week after this."

Oben kneeled on the bank and scooped some water to drink, then splashed his face, saying, "How much farther?"

Fil bent forward at the waist, then back, left and right, his bones creaking. "Not far. Listen."

In the distance, behind the whisper of the breeze in the branches, they heard the cheers of the crowd rise and fall from the tournament at Tamberlain.

Oben sipped more water from his hand. "What are we going to do when we get there?"

"We'll have to play it by ear, sonny." The aged wizard made his way to the stream, dipped a hand and drank. "We can be sure the king knows nothing about the curse, so we'll have to convince him, and that will take some improvising."

"So we just walk into the lists and say, your majesty, the man you most trust is trying to kill you with this horse?"

"If you got a better idea, I'm all ears."

Caw shook water from his feathers and said, "Naw, they're huge, but not that big."

Fil splashed at the bird, who cackled a laugh and flew away.

"The main thing is" Fil said, "you got truth on your side, so use it. Lies are Zag's stock-in-trade, not yours. Don't try to use your enemy's way. He's a master of lies, and you couldn't lie if it meant keeping your head on your shoulders. Do what you do best. Tell the truth."

Oben stood and looked over the trees toward Tamberlain. The crowd sent up a raucous cheer.

"Even if the king doesn't believe me, and has me killed anyway?"

"Even then, sonny. If that's your fate, at least you die with your honor intact."

"Yeah" Caw said with a scoffing laugh, "honor goes a long way when you're gibbeted 'til your bones bleach in the sun."

Fil scowled and said, "Fly off and scout the road, feather head."

"I wanna ride! I'm tired."

"Go tell your troubles to a priest. I left my pointy hat at home."

"Asshole" Caw grumbled and flew away.

Fil said, "Don't listen to him, kid. Remember, be-"

"I know. Be crazy."

He slapped Oben on the back. "At least you'll die happy."

Oben smiled.

"I'm gonna mosey downstream and take a leak. Be right back.

"Okay."

Oben turned again toward the capital, listening to the crowd.

Chanter lifted his head and said, "What do you think will happen to me?"

Oben turned, his look of puzzlement fading into a sad frown.

"If Zag doesn't kill me, I mean."

The man patted the horse's neck and cheek. "If we get out of this, you'll always have a home with me."

"With you and Nios, you mean?"

"Well..."

"You *are* going to marry her, right?"

"Her father will never allow-"

Chanter neighed loudly, stamped the ground and snorted, "I can't tell if you're crazy or stupid or both" he said. "If a stupid man can be crazy, or a madman stupid, then I guess you're the perfect blend of the two."

"You're a horse. You don't understand these things."

"I'm a *magic* horse, stupid madman, and I understand a lot. But it doesn't take magic to see what's plain in front of your crazy, stupid eyes. If you don't marry her, you'll die a bitter, regretful old man."

"That's if I don't die a crazy, stupid young man today."

Oben offered the stallion a sly grin.

Chanter nodded, snorted, and pushed Oben with his heavy head.

Caw suddenly alighted on a branch, agitated and squawking. "Someone's coming!"

Oben whispered, "Who?"

"Two rough-looking dudes on horseback."

"Where's Fil?"

"Dunno."

Oben made his way up the gully to the road, Chanter following, while Caw flew to a lookout high in a pine tree.

Oben whispered, "Be ready to run" and swung himself onto the horse's back.

Standing in the road, they heard slow hoofbeats and muffled talk of men.

Two of the King's Guard rode slowly around a bend. As they approached, Oben could see they were not the best of the regiment. Their white tunics were soiled, and their breastplates dull, the pink feathers in their helmets frayed and listless. Coming closer, Oben thought both the guards and the horses looked too old for the job. The men's long beards were scraggly and unkempt, matching the dirty and unbrushed manes of their mounts.

As they approached, the one Oben judged younger by his darker beard pointed and shouted, "Oi, you dere! Halt in da name o'da king."

"I'm already halted" Oben answered.

The older man laughed and spat in the dust. "Ha! A regular jester, this one is, eh Stab?"

Stab faked a laugh. "Aye, Chop, a feckin' comedian."

The soldiers stopped on either side of Oben and Chanter.

Chop said, "A comedian or a madman he is, giving sass to a King's Guard, and me with every right to cut him down cold. You a madman, boy?"

"I am Oben, of Barada."

"Well, well, well" Stab said, "just da man we lookin' for. Makes you a lucky comedian, it does."

"It does at that" Chop said and spat again. "If you wasn't the rotter we were sent for, we'd be within our *jur-is-dik-shun* to butcher you like a sow and leave the bits for the wild dogs, we would."

Stab said, "Truth told, we be sent for the horse, so maybe we can still have a bit o'fun, eh, Chop?"

"Naw, more's the pity. Zag said Otto wants the horse and the man."

Stab pulled at his beard and said, "Perhaps, but if da man was to become, like, a danger to hisself or others, an' should dat man resist all 'temps at arrest, then we'd be right in our *aw-thor-ih-tie* to slice 'im up fer dog meat, eh?"

"You have the cunning and dangerous mind of a lawyer" Chop said, smiling at his companion.

Stab smiled back. "I say we puts it to a vote. All in favor o' feeding da dogs-"

From the bushes, a woman's voice said, "Whip out his dick."

The soldiers turned right and left, their horses nervously stamping and snorting at the confusing commands.

"In the name of the king, show yourself!" Chop shouted.

From the thicket at the side of the road stepped the most beautiful red-headed woman Oben had ever seen. Tall and full-figured, her simple white peasant blouse stretched to the limit of the stitching and left little to the men's imagination. The deep green skirt waved with her swinging step, gathered and tied up to show one white, freckled thigh above the knee. Radiant curls the colors of firelight flowed over her breasts, until she tossed her head with a coquettish wink at the guards, flinging the cascade of liquid copper over her shoulder and down her back.

"Showing enough of myself, am I?" she said.

Heart-shaped, dimpled and freckled, her face was guileless as a child's while her emerald eyes flashed a harlot's promise.

The faces of the guards registered fear, then wonder, then naked desire within the space of a few heartbeats. Their beards split into wide, toothy grins of wolves stalking a fawn.

"Not as much as I might like, lass" Chop said, "but enough to know I would wish for more."

Stab pointed and said, "An' who might you be, pretty one? Out here in da scary woods of Fuckall by yerself?"

"His sister" she said, throwing the slightest glance at Oben, "so, not alone, and not scared."

"Haw" Stab laughed. "'tis pity, a pretty girl like you wif so ugly a brother."

"And what are you called, lass?" Chop asked.

"Our folks named me Filomina, but everyone calls me Filly."

Chop's smile grew wider. "Well, dear Filly, you may have just saved your brother's life, for I could not bring myself to cut a man down in the presence of so lovely a lady."

Stab lost his smile. "Come now, Chop. We kill da brother and we gets da girl to ourselves. Are ye daft, then?"

Chop glowered at his partner and said, "No more of that talk out of you, laddie. We'll follow the king's orders and bring the lot of them to his pleasure, unharmed and unmolested."

"But-"

Chop laid a hand on the hilt of his sword and said, "Not another word."

Grumbling, the junior soldier turned his mount around and said, "Well, then, let's be off."

Filly sway-stepped her way to Chop and laid a hand on his knee.

"My champion" she said, smiling up at the bewitched man, "may I ride with you?"

"An honor, dear one" Chop said, and helped her mount behind him.

She wrapped her arms around Chop's barrel chest, winked at Oben, then laid her delicate chin on his shoulder.

She whispered, "For sparing my brother's life and my virtue, glorious reward awaits you when we have time to ourselves."

Oben believed it impossible for a man to smile as broadly and gleefully as did the grizzled old warrior.

"Come then" he said, waving and turning his horse. He pointed to his dour companion and ordered, "Bring up the rear", then began a slow walk toward the sound of the cheering.

Stab mumbled unheard curses as Oben and Chanter passed him, then fell in behind.

Caw fluttered down and lighted on Oben's shoulder. He whispered, "Fil's an asshole, through and through. But good thing he's on our side."

"True words" Oben said. He watched the soldier ahead riding with his head high, delighting in the woman clinging to him and whispering vows of sensual delights. "I would not trade places with Chop for all the gold in Tamberlain."

"Yeah" Caw said, "he's a dead man."

Chapter 25 - Queens Don't Let Kings Rule Drunk

Father Sun stood high and bright in the clear blue sky, pausing for his midday meal and warming the land with his radiant benevolence.

The tournament field grew quieter in the heat as people sought refreshment and shade. Combatants finished their bouts, and King Otto honored the winners with garlands and gold. He made speeches of welcome and to whet appetites for the main event, the King's Joust, then sank back into his chair with a sigh and a belch, teetering on the edge of drunken stupor.

Now, jesters and jugglers listlessly cavorted and musicians played slow romantic tunes, while spectators sat languidly under parasols or canopies, eating and drinking, joking and flirting as the hour wore on. Knights had retired to their tents, alone or with admiring paramours, while their squires tended horses and polished armor. Peasants put the finishing touches on the lists by grooming the field and hanging colorful banners marking the contest between the two kings. Flags in the pink, white and silver of Tamberlain waved in the breeze in stark contrast with the red, black and gold of Aflax.

The kings waited with obvious impatience and growing animosity, rising from their chairs at the slightest disturbance to look for the arrival of the gift horse, then sitting again and scowling. Otto swayed unsteadily when on his feet and often barely made it to the cushioned chair to sit, drawing frightened cries from the crowd when he seemed ready to pitch headlong out of the stands and onto the field below.

Hod, stone sober, fidgeted and cursed under his breath, frustrated to distraction by the wait.

Syllabub had taken to flagrant attempts at seduction, warmed by the sun and her endless daydreams of a rough shagging from the dark king. She rubbed her shoulder against his and stroked his leg, tugging the hem of her gown upward to reveal her shapely calf.

Between her rutting and his rival's inebriation, Hod felt certain he could bend the queen over the chair and plant his first scion with her full cooperation and not a word of protest from besotted Otto.

"Must we wait for that blasted horse?" Hod finally growled.

Otto swayed and replied, "Ish a gift from my peoples..." he paused to hiccup, "...ayh mush honor the love they beshtow upon their... *shover-ine*."

"If it doesn't arrive within the hour, I say we leave off the joust and go to it straight with sword and shield."

"Yes, dear" Syllabub said with a wicked smile, "prove to this beast of a man," she batted her eyelashes at Hod, "what a brave and powerful warrior you are, all deserving of my love and... faith."

She made as if to pat her husband's shoulder with encouragement but pushed hard enough to make the crowd cry out as Otto pitched to one side, grabbed the chair and righted himself.

The people then turned their attention to the Grand Vizier's approach, announcing him with hisses and imitations of barnyard animals either fornicating or dying. He made his way onto the dais and bowed deeply.

"Where's the fucking horse, shitass?" inquired the queen.

Zag addressed Otto. "I have dispatched two of your best guardsmen to find Oben and the steed and bring them here forthwith, your majesty."

"Eschellent" the king slurred, "more wine!"

"May I suggest, my liege, that you save the wine for a celebration of your victory?"

"Schuperb idea, faithful viz... viz... Zag. Bring me ale!"

A commotion on the far side of the field drew Otto's attention away from the wine page. He stood and raised a hand to shield his eyes from the blazing sun. The queen and Hod stood and followed his gaze to an entry point between the tents where a squire appeared, yelling. The man ran across the lists toward the dais. He arrived breathless and fell to his knees before the royals, hat in hand.

"Your majesty" he panted, "your guards are coming from the Forked Road."

"My guards?" Otto said and burped, "what of them?"

Zag said, "The guardsmen I sent after the horse, your majesty."

"Ah, schplended." Otto wobbled and held out his wine cup for the page to refill. Zag lifted it from the king's hand, gave it to the page and waved the boy off.

"What about the fucking horse?" the queen demanded.

The squire said, "The guards are bringing Oben of Barada, your highness."

Hod growled, "Who in the name of Tyl's testicles is Oben of Barada?"

Zag said, "He is the talented horseman and blacksmith who trained the horse, good king."

"Schtupendous" slurred Otto, raising his empty hand to his mouth and drinking the air.

Hod asked the squire, "But what about the horse?"

"The horse is coming, King Hod."

"Well... When?"

"When the guards arrive, dear king."

Zag took over. "You mean when they bring Oben of Barada?"

"Yes, your, your... vizierness."

The queen fumed, "Why in the fuck should it matter when Oben of Barada gets here?"

The squire flinched under the queen's gaze. "Because the horse comes with Oben of Barada on his back, my queen."

Syllabub and Hod shouted in unison, "That's all one!"

Otto raised his empty hand in salute, shouted "Huzzscha!" and fell back into the chair.

Zag, hearing this news, said nothing. His already pale complexion drained from eggshell to that of freshly fallen snow.

A great cheer rose from the crowd as Chop slow-walked his mount onto the field, Filly still clinging to his back, followed by Oben on the beautiful white stallion. Stab entered last, his horse carrying its head low and woeful as its rider. They crossed the lists and approached the royal dais, Chop moving left and Stab right.

Oben led Chanter forward between the two guards. Without a word or touch, he stopped the horse near the dais and bowed in greeting as Chanter nodded his noble head and neighed loudly.

Zag stared at Oben, his face regaining its color as his eyes hardened in anger.

"Your beloved majesty, King Otto, I am Oben of Barada, your humble servant."

Otto struggled to his feet. "Welcome good Oben, I see you have brought my horsshe, Thunderhoovesesh."

"Ah, uh, well, he prefers the name Chanter, Your Majesty."

"He does? How do you know that?"

"I know horses, great king."

Otto grinned and staggered against his wife's shoulder, slurring, "I like thish fellow, he has schpunk."

Syllabub pushed him off and waved her hand to fan the air.

"I thank you" Otto said, "and all the people of Barada for this gra... gra..." he belched, "grahcheous gift."

"My king" Oben said, "you have been deceived. This horse is not a gift from the people of Barada."

The crowd murmured and whispered. Syllabub frowned, and Hod scowled.

Otto said, "What do you mean?" The king pointed to the magician and almost fell over from the momentum, "My trusted vizh-ish-ier told me the people of Bah... Bah... Barada made a gift of it to me, and that you trained it, schpecially for the Kings's's Jousht."

Oben nodded. "As I say, beloved king, you have been deceived." Oben glared at Zag, who returned the look with double the venom. "By that very man himself, Grand Vizier Zag."

The crowd gasped.

Syllabub scowled.

Hod gritted his teeth and grumbled.

Zag's face burned redder with every word.

"The horse is not from Barada, King Otto, and was not trained by me. It is a horse hexed by Zag, who put a spell on the poor creature that will result in your death here today!"

The crowd buzzed.

Syllabub gasped.

Hod grinned.

"And yours as well" Oben said, pointing, "King Hod of Aflax."

Hod gaped and bellowed, "What?"

Zag raised his arms and shouted, his voice echoing across the field, "Hear me, oh great kings."

The crowd, Syllabub and Hod fell silent.

Otto belched.

The pale, gaunt magician said, "I have told you recently, beloved king, of plots arising from rebels in Barada, have I not?"

Otto's face blanched. "You ha... have, good wizherd."

"My suspicions have been proven, and now we see these foul designs come to fruition. The horse and it's training, seemingly so innocent, are but parts of a clever ruse to undermine you here today. Oben is the ringleader, and I'll have him confessing his guilt before he takes his next breath!"

He raised his arms and shouted, "Bring in the traitor's wife!"

A page led a simple wooden cart, drawn by a fat and a thin donkey, from behind the stands. The animals grunted and brayed under the weight, and the wheels creaked as it made its way toward the dais.

The boy stopped the cart directly below the royals and ran away.

In the flat bed of the cart lay Nios, arms and legs splayed and bound to the planks, the red gown taut over her curves, her mouth stopped with a torturous gag.

Helpless, her eyes flashed molten, defiant fury at Zag. Then they turned to Oben and melted with unrestrained devotion.

Oben could not breathe for some moments, his heart burning, his mind screaming to make whatever capitulation would free her from bondage.

Zag pointed and intoned, "Here is the co-conspirator, your majesty, the wife of Oben, who together with him and the people of Barada have hatched this diabolical scheme to bring you down and put Hod on the throne of Tamberlain!"

Otto staggered and held his hand to his lips.

"And now" Zag went on, "I will force from this Oben himself a confession of his crimes, and the names of his rabble compatriots, or..." he paused and looked again on Nios, "or he can watch as I flay the tender flesh from his beloved's bones, slowly, carefully, so that death will never release her from her agony until I choose to sever her lovely head from her shoulders."

The magician swept his hand at Nios as if wielding a blade. A short, thin gash appeared on her arm, a bright red line that oozed blood, making her cry out against the gag.

People in the crowd gasped, screamed, and cursed.

Syllabub fainted into Hod's arms.

Hod gaped at Zag in abject fear.

Otto sat heavily in the chair, dropped his head between his knees, and vomited.

Chapter 26 - The Kings' Joust or Something Like It

The commotion in the grandstands reached a panicked pitch at the sight of the incapacitated king, lying on the dais in his own spew, his wife in the arms of the rival king, and the evil magician reveling in his power with glowing eyes, arms raised and ready to strike like a two-legged cobra.

Women screamed, and men fainted. Half-dressed and sweating knights left their tents and ran into the field. Squires fled as their horses neighed and reared.

The tableau held for a time: royals and vizier, guards with shocked faces, Oben sitting Chanter, and captive Nios bleeding and struggling, before the commotion finally quieted.

Hod seated the queen and revived her, and with no other ruler fully cognizant, took charge.

"What does this man mean, Zag" the dark king said, "accusing you of planning to kill both Otto and me?"

The vizier hesitated, his powerful stare at Nios weakening, his words faltering. "I... he... Oben and his bitch are the traitorous ones, great king" he stammered. "They and all of Barada should be... be... destroyed to the... last... mewling babe."

Zag quieted and faltered, seeming to lose strength of breath.

He did not notice the hard gaze from the comely redhead seated behind Chop, nor distinguish the spell of confusion the disguised old man directed at his black heart.

"I have proof!" Oben shouted, holding the arrow aloft, the red ribbon around the damning letter fluttering in the wind. "Proof of Zag's diabolical plan to kill the kings and become emperor of both lands!"

The fire of Tyl's Inferno returned to the magician's eyes. "Lying peasant! You will watch me butcher your woman before I burn you alive as kindling for your entire clan!"

Hod shouted, "Guards!"

Three massive men in black armor appeared from behind the dais and surrounded their sovereign.

"Keep that slimy snake of a man in check" he ordered.

The men ran to Zag and surrounded him. Two grabbed his arms and pinioned him while the third held the blade of a dagger at his thin, pale throat.

Revived and angry, Syllabub rose and shouted, "Guards!"

Three stout men in silver breastplates rushed to their queen's side.

"Make sure Hod's men don't harm the vizier... until I give the order."

The three men of Tamberlain drew their swords and held them ready, standing close behind each of the Aflax soldiers.

Held hostage, Zag's face paled and fell into a helpless frown, but only a moment passed before confidence reappeared on his face.

Syllabub gestured to Oben. "What is this proof you claim, Oben of Barada?"

"This letter, your highness, written in Zag's own hand. It orders me to deliver this horse, and to act as squire to King Otto, helping him to mount for the joust."

Hod said, "What of it? I hear no evil plan in that."

"Anyone who rides this horse faster than a walk will die."

Hod stared a heartbeat, then laughed, "You seem healthy enough."

"I know horses" Oben answered.

Hod shook his head. "Preposterous."

"It's true" Oben said. "Zag ordered me to ensure Otto rode this horse in the joust. He would walk to the lists without harm, but as soon as he spurred, he would die, and you would become king."

With these words, Oben saw the shock of understanding on the king's face. "And I would then ride him in victory" he breathed.

"Yes, and you would surely die."

Zag laughed, making the guards tighten their hold. "He calls this proof? He lies to save himself and his slut. I will kill them both with great pain in service to your royal prerogative, gracious queen and king."

"Well?" the queen said to Oben. "What real proof can you give of this wild claim?"

Filly rose in the saddle from behind Chop. "My brave champion will disprove this vile liar's accusations!" she shouted.

The queen frowned at the redhead.

Hod smiled at her.

Oben gave Fil-within-Filomina a sideways glance.

Filly-who-was-Fil winked back.

"Who is this kitchen slave?" the queen asked.

"I am Oben's sister" Filly said, "and I know he is lying. This brave man, guardsman Chop, will ride the horse and prove the lie my brother tells, staining our family's honor."

"I will?" whispered Chop.

Filly kissed the gruff man's cheek, then cooed sweetly in his ear, "Yes, you will my love, for you are brave and virile, and I am yours entirely when you prove your love for me."

Chop's dour, bearded face blossomed into a lustful smile.

"Well, Guardsman?" the queen said. "will you take this risk, for your sovereign's sake?"

"Aye, beloved queen, I will."

Chop helped Filly down, then dismounted. He went to Chanter as Oben slid from the great beast's back.

"We have no saddle for him" Oben said, "if you can ride without."

Chop scoffed and growled, "Whelp, I was riding horses bareback when the best part of you was running down your mammy's thigh."

Weighted down with armor and weapons, he struggled to jump and get a leg over the horse's croup. Oben acted the squire and boosted the big man into place.

Chop gently squeezed Chanter's ribs to urge him into a walk. As he turned in a tight circle, the man let his face relax from worry to smiling confidence.

Oben said, "Trot."

With a gentle nudge, Chanter broke into a working trot. The rider smiled through the first familiar rhythm of one-two, one-two hoofbeats. Suddenly, his face froze in a grotesque grimace of pain, his muscles seized, and he slid from his seat to land with a sickening thud in the dirt of the arena.

The crowd again gasped and cried out.

Syllabub raised her delicate fingers to cover her gaping mouth.

Hod's eyes shot open, then narrowed in anger.

Chanter calmly walked to Oben.

"That is no proof!" Zag cried out, struggling against the hold of the men. "Mere coincidence. No doubt Ludd wrote this moment of the man's death in his book back when He formed the world!"

Filly ran to Stab's side and gripped him by the thigh.

"Please" she said, her hands reaching toward his codpiece, "You must help me! I will be without family, without a home if this man prevails. Please, prove this falsehood and I will be yours, body and heart, for as long as I live!"

Stab smiled at the luscious redhead, but then looked at his friend's corpse and lost his color.

Filly reached higher on his leg, her eyes full of rich promise, and whispered, "When this is finished, drag me to a tent and take me like you own me, for you will."

Stab paused only a heartbeat, then smiled and dismounted.

Filly took the man's hand and pressed it to her considerable bosom.

Stab squeezed her hard, kissed her deeply, and went to Chanter. He dropped his weapons as he approached and waved Oben away. Leaping to seat himself, he quickly urged the horse to walk.

All eyes followed his easy turns. He passed by Filly and gave her a wink before he spurred the animal's flank.

All eyes watched him stiffen, gurgle in his throat and slip sideways off the horse, burying his face into the manure-laden soil.

As Stab's last gasp escaped his slackened jaw, every human witness fell silent, incapable of movement or sound.

Only Chanter's slow steps and his breathing broke the silence as he returned to where Oben stood and accepted the man's calming touch.

Hod was the first to recover. He turned his glower on Zag, then caught sight of Syllabub watching him, her own face a gathering storm of rage. With the slightest secret, silent meeting of their eyes, the king and queen sealed a living pact.

He broke from his new beloved's gaze and looked down regally on the magician, trapped by three men guarded by three more men. He took a deep breath to ready for a damning proclamation, but Zag beat him to it.

"Enough!" the magician screamed.

His word echoed from Mount Tamberlain, from the walls of the castle, from the ravines of the rivers and from the faraway caldera of Mount Fire.

Zag's eyes rolled back as he turned his pale face to the sky and intoned, "*Alys fold hoy tut! Gamine reeky vet!*"

Silence. Stillness. All the world immobile as if rendered a mural painting on the very air.

The people in the stands froze where they stood, faces a thousand reactions of shock and fear. The squires and knights and horses in the lists stood like statues in a park. The trees and banners no longer waved in the wind, stopped as if encased in amber.

Chanter stepped back nervously and snorted. Oben patted the horse's neck and said, "Easy."

He glanced at Filly, who met his eye with wary curiosity and nodded.

He looked to Nios, still bound and gagged. She slowly closed and opened her eyes in salute and managed a brave smile from behind the gag.

It seemed only Oben, Nios, Filly and Chanter remained breathing, mobile, sensate.

Until the voice again rose from the magician, quietly repeating his command in the low growl of a tree cat ready to strike, "Enough."

The three immobile soldiers holding Zag shattered like brittle glass and rained in shards onto the boards of the dais.

Freed, he reached out to each of the guards in silver and tapped them with a long, thin finger. Like the others, each man broke into a thousand pieces and fell like hail onto the wooden slats.

"Now" Zag said, his smile triumphant, "time for your reckoning."

Chapter 27 - Careful Where You Point That Thing

The Grand Vizier raised his arms, making the long, loose sleeves of his robe spread like wings, and with a simple wave lifted himself into the air. He flew over the grandstand fence and floated down to land near the cart.

Chanter nickered and stamped a foot. Oben, staring at the magician, patted the horse's neck and murmured to calm him.

Filly stepped back once, then twice, her pleasing face tightening in rising hot anger.

Zag walked to the cart and stood over the bound woman in red. He looked down at her and smiled.

From her eyes to his, she screamed a thousand silent, blistering curses. His smile grew.

"A hero's choice" he hissed, "that is what you said, wasn't it, lovely storyteller?"

"Leave her be" Oben said. "It's me you want."

Zag laughed and said to Nios, "How patently heroic, how predictable, how cliché, don't you think? When you said your Oben would make a hero's choice, is this what you meant? He would ruin every chance for your happiness, condemn you to torturous death, then try to assuage his guilt with brave-sounding words?"

Nios struggled against her bonds and growled from behind the gag, making the magician laugh more.

"The two of you could have lived long and bountiful lives in my court. Riches beyond compare, a passel of children and grandchildren to cushion your age, a legacy to offer them at your passing. Your deep love over scores of years could have been the very food to sustain your souls both here and the hereafter."

The vizier raised his eyes from Nios to Oben. "Instead, you made a hero's choice, just as she said you would. You made the choice you thought righteous, moral, courageous. And for what? You will lose even yet. I will have what is mine, all Tamberlain, and Aflax, and all of Moa one day. You have delayed my plans, not ended them."

He looked again at Nios, her eyes now glistening with the tears she struggled to hide.

"Having lost what you sought to save, you lose the one thing that should have mattered most to you. Her."

He reached down and gently brushed her reddened cheek with the back of his thin, icy fingers.

"I tell you this, hero. If a woman loved me as she loves you, I would lie and steal, cheat and kill to keep her safe and in my arms. I would give up every worldly desire, debase my every scruple, condemn myself to a life of sin and an eternity of penance if that's what would make her mine and keep her mine."

A fire rose in Oben's throat. He gripped the arrow in his right hand, dreaming of driving it deep into the magician's chest to stop the words that found their mark in his heart.

"And you" Zag said as he straightened to look at Oben with a face of sorrow, "you could not even hold your tongue and let two foolish men meet their just fates. Not even that."

Oben saw Filly from the corner of his eye raise her hands toward the magician and begin an incantation, "*Cerf du-*"

Zag thrust his palm at Filly and glared into her deep green eyes.

The redhead froze, held by the magician's will, grimacing in pain.

"I see your ugly, wrinkled hide behind that pretty face, Fil" Zag said. "I told you before never to cross me again, didn't I? Yes, I did. Too bad you didn't heed my warning."

Zag drew his arm back and with a sharp push sent Filly flying across the lists for a hundred yards before slamming her to the ground. She lay where she landed, unmoving.

Oben watched as Filly slowly faded away to reveal an unconscious Fil sprawled in the dirt. He heard Zag laugh again, low and menacing, and turned back to him with burning eyes.

"You sealed your fate when you joined up with that third-rate conjurer" Zag said. "I'll bet he said you could wield magic yourself."

Oben said, "Think it, and it happens."

"Fool" Zag laughed. "It's not your mind that makes magic." He suddenly shouted, "It's your heart!"

As casually as taking hold of a doll, Zag reached out to Oben and cupped his hand. Oben felt the grip take his entire body and squeeze until he could barely gulp breath.

"Please, come closer" Zag said, and drew his arm in, dragging Oben across the arena until he stood by the cart over Nios.

"I want you to have a front-row seat to this part of the show. Watch what happens to the woman you love when you make" he sneered as he spoke, "*a hero's choice.*"

A sweep of his free hand tore the bodice of the gown away, exposing her breasts. The twitch of a finger drew a tiny gush of blood near her nipple. Another pass and a line dripped red at the hollow of her throat.

Nios cried out with each wound, then fought to keep from Zag the pleasure he sought in her surrender.

"Death of a thousand cuts, they call it" Zag said, gloating. "I can do this all day, and I will!"

Zag's eyes now blazed with bloodlust. He waved his hand to draw the gown up and with three flicks of his wrist cut a six-pointed star of crimson on her creamy white thigh.

"Keep in mind" Zag said, his voice now guttural with excitement, "once I finish flaying her to the bones, you're next."

A high screech echoed across the lists as Caw landed on Zag's shoulder and flapped wildly. He pecked at the magician's cheek, aiming to reach his eyes, sending Zag staggering back and flailing at the murderous bird.

The distraction freed Oben. Before he could react, Chanter snorted and charged the cursing vizier as Caw flew off. The horse reared and kicked at Zag, his equine screams shifting into language and back again.

"Neiihggh! I'll kill you, bastard! Stomp you to... neeiiggh! Die, neeiigh!"

Zag retreated further, narrowly escaping the sledgehammer hooves Chanter aimed at his head.

The panicked vizier managed to throw a spell to hold the charging animal back, but not enough to keep him still. Chanter slowly closed the distance, lowering his head and digging in as if pulling a heavy wagon.

Fil had recovered and ran toward the battle, staggering and panting, both arms outstretched. He threw his own holding spell on Zag, making him grimace in pain and eye the rival wizard with murderous intent.

Oben could see and hear the magic energy, the air sparking and crackling between them, Zag holding Chanter at bay, Fil holding Zag hostage and draining his power.

Struggling, Fil shouted, "The arrow!"

The words shook Oben from his stupor, but he balked in confusion.

"The arrow" Fil repeated, "the archer's bow!"

The words reached Oben and spurred him to run to the cart. He found Flap's bow and took it up, notching the arrow on the string.

Nios gazed into his eyes and smiled. He pulled the cruel gag away and gently kissed her lips.

Parting only a touch, he made as if to speak, but she whispered, her breath sweet and warm against him, "I know."

He smiled and ran toward the fray.

Zag was splitting his strength between the horse and Fil, weakening the short wizard's magic but also his own, allowing Chanter to gain ground.

Oben stopped near the battle, took the vial of potion from his satchel and poured the brew over the arrowhead. He threw the bottle away and raised the bow, drawing the string taut and aiming for Zag's heart.

Fil screamed and strained to the limit of his power, taking Zag by surprise and breaking his hold on Chanter.

As Oben loosed, the horse lunged at the magician. The arrow whistled through the charged air and pierced Chanter's shoulder.

The great animal screamed and reared, blood pouring from the wound. He broke off and thundered across the field.

Oben stood as if stone, watching Chanter gallop away.

Freed from one attack, Zag turned his fury on Fil, both hands sending deadly magic at him, his face aglow with triumph.

Fil staggered, faltering, losing the energy to hold back his foe.

The laugh from the vizier shook Oben's bones.

"I warned you, and now I make good on that warning!"

Oben saw Zag raise a fist as if to hammer Fil into the ground. He screamed, ran across the field and with all his strength batted the vizier's head with the bow.

The strike was just enough to break the spell and make Zag lose his footing. Holding his head, he stumbled to one knee, then stared into Oben's eyes.

Oben felt an icy hand grip his heart and clutch until the beating slowed. His knees buckled. He crumpled into the dirt and sighed what he knew was his last breath. The world dimmed.

A low moan, rising to a bone-chilling scream, shook the ground, rattled the boards of the dais, rocked the trees at their roots.

His vision fading, Oben sought the source of the sound.

Chanter's body convulsed as the animal bayed again in agony, the low bellow of a thousand slaughtered cattle rising to the skull-aching shriek of a million butchered lambs. Oben watched the animal transform, the bones of his legs cracking as they morphed in shape and angle. The rear legs fattened and bent back, dropping the haunch to the ground while the chest grew impossibly wide, and the forelegs shortened.

Fil roused and watched the strange metamorphosis.

Zag, too, eased his hold on Oben and stared in fascination.

As the cries and screams pierced their ears, they watched Chanter's head lose its equine features and take on the wide, flat skull and broad, razor-toothed mouth of a dragon. The neck stretched, as did the tail, morphing from hair to flesh and elongating, thick at the rump and tapering to a point, growing sharp plates along the spine. The silken white coat bubbled, cockled and discolored into a mottled mixture of scales, flesh and feathers. Massive, leathery wings sprouted from his shoulders, growing twice his length and beating the air so powerfully they kicked dust into the men's eyes.

With a final trumpeting cry, Chanter reared on his thickly muscled back legs and pushed himself skyward. The wings took over and lifted him away, past the men and over the grandstand. He rose above the treetops and turned back toward the lists, his call now that of a hundred eagles in chorus with a lion's roar.

The massive beast dove from his height, eyes blazing, the great clawed talons of the back legs spread wide.

Zag raised his hand in a futile gesture and screamed as Chanter clutched his trunk in one claw and pulled again for the sky.

One wing beat, two, three, and the monster that was Chanter reached a hundred feet above the ground. He took another turn back over the men, the cart, and the dais. Oben and Fil heard Zag screaming curses at Chanter, at them, at the turn of fate as he passed.

One last wide, banking gyre and Chanter soared again toward the arena, wings splayed and motionless, gliding on the wind.

Speeding closer, Zag shouted unintelligible incantations. He freed one arm, plucked a feather from Chanter's leg and cast it down. It fluttered in the wake of the beast's flight and then floated slowly toward the ground.

"Still you fail, hero!" Zag shouted from overhead.

Oben and Fil sat in the dust, watching Chanter's great wings beat the air slowly, carrying him higher and faster with every stroke. They heard Zag scream his agony in the crushing grip of the talon.

As beast and man shrank into the distance, Oben saw Chanter's path would take them to the smoldering, smoky crest of Mount Fire.

A shout from Nios, "Oben!", roused him. He clambered to his feet and watched the feather flutter and dive until the quill stabbed her near the heart. The pinprick of a wound would be nothing without the evil spell it carried from Zag's blackened soul.

Nios expelled her last breath and died.

Chapter 28 - Foreplay for a Long Time

Oben shouted, "Nios!" and ran to the cart. He freed her hands and feet and lifted the bodice of her gown to restore her modesty, whispering her name gently as if rousing her from a pleasant nap.

Her eyes remained closed, her breath stilled. Oben cried her name, then shook her by the shoulders and screamed her name.

Fil stood opposite and saw the truth of it reach Oben's heart. The would-be hero stared at his lover's face with glazed eyes, clenching his jaw to fight down the rising fire in his throat.

The rest of the world remained frozen by Zag's spell, still and silent as death itself.

Glancing at faces in the crowd, Fil saw life in their eyes. Theirs was a bondage, not death, and he could see they had witnessed everything, and watched even now. The magician's spell held them, but did not kill them, or blind them, or steal their sense.

Having seen the great battle with Zag, they all now bore silent witness to the man crushed by heartbreak, standing over his beloved's lifeless body, keening her loss with the ancient, animal grief of bone-deep pain.

Fil's own mournful face changed, lifted, until he grinned broadly and said, "He fucked up."

Oben looked at Fil, tears streaming, teeth bared, his brow furrowed. "What?"

"Zag fucked up" Fil repeated. He rushed around the cart to stand by Nios, pressed the fingers of his left hand to her throat and his right over her heart.

Oben screamed, "Get away from her!" and pushed Fil so hard he stumbled.

"No, idiot! Don't you get it?"

Fil scrambled to his feet and elbowed Oben aside. He again checked her throat and her heart, closing his eyes and mumbling.

"Get what?"

Fil's eyes sprang open, and he smiled. "She's not dead!"

Oben stopped breathing, then wiped the tears with his sleeve and whispered, "Not dead?"

"Well, she's dead, but not *dead* dead."

"What in Ludd's name does that mean?"

"You know how sometimes a girl will say she likes you, but she doesn't *like you* like you?"

Oben thought a moment. "No."

"No? That's never happened to you?"

"No."

"Huh, lucky bastard."

"Don't lie to me, Fil, not now."

"No lie, sonny, I mean every word. Somehow, that miserable shit Zag messed up his spells. Look at the people."

Oben followed Fil's pointing finger and gazed at the crowd. Like Fil, he saw they were awake, their eyes sparkling with awareness, trapped within immobile flesh.

"What does that have to do with Nios?" Oben said.

"Zag meant to keep everyone from seeing what he was doing, but he failed. He meant to kill Nios, but he failed at that, too."

"She's not really dead?"

"Not *dead* dead, no. You can revive her."

"How?"

"Give her what she's always wanted. Marry her."

"But" Oben stammered and scanned the crowd, "There's no priest."

Fil sighed, "Tyl's balls, sonny, are you really that dumb?"

"What do I do Fil? Tell me, please!"

"You don't marry her with a priest, in a church. You marry her with your heart."

"My heart?"

"And... your... body."

Oben shook his head, struggling to make sense of Fil's words.

"You know" Fil said, glancing downward.

"No Fil, I don't know, I don't understand what you're saying."

"Sheesh, kids these days, I tell ya."

"Fil?"

The magician cleared his throat and said, "You know. Shake the sheets, amorous congress, a bit of how's yer father, give the dog a bone."

Oben gaped at Fil, his forehead furrowed.

"The old in-out? Hide the sausage? Wet the willy? Plant the parsnip? Jam the clam?"

Oben grabbed the short man by the shoulders and shook him. "Tell me, Fil!"

Fil pulled himself away just as Caw landed on his shoulder and screeched, "Fuck the girl, you dim sonofabitch!"

Oben gasped, "What? Here? Now?"

Fil frowned. "Maybe you want to wait until she's *dead* dead? That's illegal in Tamberlain."

Oben looked from Fil to Nios, to Fil, to the crowd and back to Nios.

"Remember, sonny" Fil said, sympathy warming his face, "when all else fails, be crazy."

Oben said, "I'll kiss her. That will bring her back."

Caw still on his shoulder, Fil walked to the other side of the cart and said, "You been reading too many story books, kid."

Oben bent down and kissed Nios on the lips, a gesture loving but chaste.

"Fer Ludd's sake" Fil said, "she's not your maiden aunt. Kiss her for real!"

"For real?"

"Tongue, clod-brain, give her some tongue."

Oben again kissed Nios and gently pressed his tongue between her lips. For a moment, the gates of her teeth remained locked, but then the softest sigh from her sweetened the air as she opened to his probing. He explored her mouth, tongue to tongue, feeling the faintest response. The familiar touch and taste of her, warm and open to his desire, heated the blood in his belly. His breath came fast and shallow.

"Whoo, boy" Fil whispered.

Caw sang, "Bow chick a wow wow."

Oben held her face in his hands as his desire rose and his tongue plunged deeper. He wrapped the tendrils of her hair in his fingers, broke from her mouth and planted soft, wet pecks on her closed eyelids, her smooth forehead, her cool but still rosy cheeks.

"Squeeze her titties" Fil groaned.

Oben glanced at the magician, now rubbing himself through his rough woolen robe.

Fill grinned sheepishly, "Please?"

Oben cupped one full, round breast in his hand through the torn bodice of her gown. He felt the spot where she had bled, and his eyes welled at the memory of her pain. He drew the thin red cloth down and pressed his lips to the wound near her nipple, licking it slowly. The blood, stopped since Zag cursed her with death, dripped again, and he hungrily drew it into his mouth, taking in the nipple as well and sucking lightly.

Eyes still closed, Nios drew a labored breath. The sign of life thrilled Oben, now dizzy with yearning. His mouth and tongue and hands kissed, licked, and fondled both her breasts as he had done so many times before, knowing what touch delighted her. Another deep inhale from her made him moan, his thirst for her mixed with the pang of hope in his chest that she would live.

A quiet word from Fil, "Oben?" and he forced himself to lift his head, his eyesight blurry.

"She needs more, sonny. More!"

"*I* need more" Caw whispered.

He moved to kiss her lips softly while his hand pulled the hem of the gown upward. He glanced down, his breath balking at the shock of her beauty. He laid his palm on her belly and slid downward, over the sleek black hair, and with two fingers gently pressed the moist bud of her flower.

The touch drew a gasp from her and the slightest arch of her hips. The thrill in Oben's heart sent heated blood to his root, making his swollen phallus ache for freedom. Breathing in ragged gulps, he worked her cleft in circles from apex to nadir, quickening as he felt her wetness rise.

Nios now parted her lips and sighed, then drew breath in quick gasps. Oben returned to gently kissing her warming mouth as his fingers danced over, around, in and out, a *pas de deux* they had practiced and perfected over many years.

The sound of her laboring to live, the slippery feel of her on his fingertips, the turgid throb in his own loins drew Oben's mouth down from hers, pausing again to kiss each swollen nipple, then move on past her navel. His tongue skated over her rounded mount until it joined his fingers in the salty folds of her sex.

Her eyes still closed, Nios moaned openly and lifted her hand in a weak gesture. It brushed Oben's auburn locks then fell again at her side. But strength returned to her hips, and she lifted and lowered herself along his probing lips and tongue, the rhythm now answering his pace.

Fil and Caw stared, dumbfounded with longing. Fil had reached inside his robe and was stroking himself furiously, his face scrunched with frustrated enjoyment.

Caw said, "By Ludd, I wish I had hands."

Now panting, Oben climbed onto the cart and kneeled between his love's parted legs, to pleasure her in a way they'd learned would make her peak with joy. Licking and sucking at her sensitive nub, he plunged two fingers deep within, making her push herself down to drive him farther and drawing her first word, a sighing, "Oh!".

Oben hooked his fingers inside and worked them like a lute player, the rhythm speeding, the notes of their breathy song rising in chorus. Now he moaned into her quim, growing mad with the hope in his heart and his aching cock that strained against the prison wall of his trousers.

Caw suddenly screeched and flapped his wings, shouting, "Chanter! No!"

A bright ball of light flashed across the sky, fiery red and yellow, followed in seconds by a ground-shaking explosion.

Shocked, Oben lifted his head from the center of the universe, and Fil stopped waxing his carrot.

The men and the bird all stared to the east, where a massive mushroom of flame and smoke grew from the chimney of Mount Fire and climbed skyward. The ground continued to shake and rumble in aftershocks while molten, liquid rock overflowed the lip of the caldera and oozed slowly down the mountain. The cloud of smoke and ash darkened as it rose, threatening to overtake the Father and blanket the land in shadow.

"Oh, Ludd" Fil gasped.

Oben let sense return and said, "Fil? What was that?"

"Zag's dead" Fil whispered.

"And Chanter" Caw said.

"Yeah."

"What?"

Fil pointed east. "Chanter must have sacrificed himself in Mount Fire, taking Zag with him. It's the only way to make sure that evil fuck is dead and gone forever."

Oben's eyes welled. "Chanter too? You're sure."

Fil glanced at Caw on his shoulder. They both said, "Yes."

As the thunder of the explosion died away, Fil and Oben heard voices. The people in the grandstand, released from their captivity, staggered about in a daze but smiled, laughed, and greeted their equally lucky friends. The knights and squires in the arena stretched sore limbs and called out to their friends while horses and dogs gamboled about celebrating their liberty.

Kneeling over Nios, still trapped in the evil spell, Oben said, "Are you sure Zag's dead?"

"His magic has been destroyed. See the people? They're free!"

Looking over the crowd again, it was obvious to Oben that the people had watched the erotic display between himself and Nios, and the echo of his still smoldering lust was singing in their bones. The lords and ladies, merchants and wives, lovers and friends began pairing off to embrace, kiss and fondle. Some looked back at the cart, smiled at the bawdy spectacle and went back to making their partners laugh and swoon with delight at their insistent touch.

He looked at Fil with pleading eyes. "But what about her?"

The wizard looked down on Nios and said, "He cast a special spell on her, sonny. Only you can break it."

Untouched for some time, they watched as her breathing quieted and slowed. The tiny movements of her hips and hands stilled. Oben laid a hand on her naked thigh and felt the flesh cooling. Zag's deadly curse on her had not abated. Drawn up only halfway from the abyss, Nios was swiftly falling back to her doom.

Fil said, "You know what you've gotta do, lover boy, and you better hurry. Now is when you really make a hero's choice."

Chapter 29 - Just Enough People for an Orgy

O ben cried out, a quiet "No!", and stretched his body over his dying beloved. He covered her unbreathing mouth with his, desperate to rouse her again.

She responded to his hungry kiss, lips quivering. A weak moan escaped her throat into his, and he echoed it with his own cry, a mix of thirst and anguish.

Plunging his hand between her legs again, he rubbed and pushed wantonly, too crazed with libido and misery to touch her with finesse. When she did not stir, he slowed his feverish caress, laid his face in her rich black hair and sobbed.

A puff of breath warmed Oben's ear as Nios roused slightly and whispered, "Please."

He remained lost in the forest of her tresses.

Again she breathed in his ear, "Please" as she reached one hand weakly to his waist.

Feeling her movement, Oben lifted himself and watched as her delicate fingers pushed past his belt into his trousers. He felt them reach the tip of his erect manhood and gently press, sending sparks down the shaft and tightening his taint in anticipation.

"Please" she breathed, low and guttural, and again, "Please."

On the dais, King Otto lay moaning on the floor, struggling to rouse from the effects of magic and wine.

Syllabub and Hod had shaken off the remnants of the spell and stood hugging and smiling. Having watched the sad but arousing spectacle below them, still wrapped in each other's arms, they turned to gaze at each other. In seconds, merriment melted into arousal. Their embrace turned intimate, and their eyes spoke what their bodies felt.

Hod suddenly clutched the queen's thick, flaxen hair with one hand and roughly kissed her as the other took possessive hold of her breast. Her knees gave way, but she held tight to his shoulders, pressed her thighs against his and abdicated the throne of her virtue to the bearded marauder assaulting her citadel.

Below, Nios had set alight the bonfire of Oben's searing lust. It overcame his senses and his fears, burning away everything in the world except his need to meld with her. He tugged wildly at his pants to free himself. Rising to his knees, he pulled her thighs around his and lifted her hips to open her fully. One hand spread her fleshy petals while the other aimed his swollen lingam. With a swift thrust he pierced her as far as flesh allowed, then pressed harder, madly seeking the union of two into one flesh.

Anchored in his beloved, motionless save a pulsing at the root of his stalk, he lifted his face to the sky and bellowed like a rutting elk.

Nios still did not open her eyes, but she gasped a deep, struggling breath and let it out with a long cry of unutterable joy.

The dark king and the fair queen had broken off their fevered kissing long enough to watch the moment of the young couple's joining. With a breathy groan, Syllabub pushed back from Hod's embrace and dropped to her knees. She yanked his codpiece open, freed his hard, reddened phallus and thrust it hungrily into her mouth.

Nios quickened and reached out to push Oben at the hips, urging him to pull back. He did, and just as the crown of his scepter was about to leave her bereft, he plunged back into her depths. They both shouted their joy as Oben re-chambered slowly, reversed and pierced her again.

Beyond himself with bliss, knowing at last why Nios begged him to join with her in this way, Oben reveled in the sensations of withdrawal and advance, slowly at first then speeding his pace.

The sight and sound of the young couple's thrilling moment of coupling intoxicated the crowd with delirious carnality. People pulled at their own clothes to free groin and buttock and chest or tore at garments blocking them from caressing whoever was close at hand. Pairs formed up and joined one body part to another, then morphed into threesomes as someone claimed an unoccupied bit of flesh.

On the field, a knight took hold of his smiling squire, wrestled him to the ground and then quickly robbed him of his breeches and pierced him with a long, fat erection. The younger man squealed with delight and urged his master to ride him like a steed into battle.

Soon, Oben was pounding himself into Nios with hard, fast thrusts, sounding a bestial grunt with every stroke. She echoed his rhythm with her hips and her plaintive squeals, kicking her heels at his haunches to spur him to full gallop, racing to reach the edge of the world.

He hovered his face over hers, drinking in her honeyed breath as she gasped his name with every hammer blow to her core, "Oben! Oben! Oben!"

The frenzy of fornication and frottage surrounding their wooden, wheeled wedding bed grew in complexity and cacophonous volume with every racing heartbeat.

The knight buggering his squire in the dust of the lists was now taking a double-buggering at both ends by two equally lust-crazed guardsmen.

In the stands, one enterprising lady of the court was doing her best to satisfy three men and a woman while a fourth male hovered with a ready cock in hand, alert for an opening.

Nearby, one overly lucky fellow had somehow corralled a harem of three lovely ladies, bottoms up in a line. He disappointed all three by slipping his pud into one, then the other, then the third before returning for another round. When two of his friends came to the rescue and clocked in for cock duty, all six quickly formed a chorus line of deep-and-hard synchronized fuckery, happily grunting and yelping in unison.

An imaginative foursome worked out the calculus involved and were crying with delight as the women, lying reversed together to gulp each other's pink pearls, also enjoyed impressive, flesh-slapping cocksmanship from two well-equipped and muscled soldiers of Aflax.

Stallions chased mares, donkeys and other stallions around the arena. Dogs howled in dick-stretched, passionate agony while cats tussled as hissing, screeching pinwheels of pain.

As sovereigns must do for their people, Syllabub and Hod were setting the gold standard example for growling, wild-eyed, saliva-spattered horse fucking. Bent deeply over the arm of Hod's chair, the queen clamped the embroidered seat cushion in her teeth and joyously grunted a lungful of air with each deep, womb-shaking, ball-bouncing thrust from the dark king. Delivering the goods with a pounding that shook the dais, Hod gripped her wrists with one bear-paw hand, her thick blond locks with the other and huffed like a rutting bull, eyes rolled back and face to the sky.

Otto had recovered and sat in the far chair quietly rubbing himself through his silken trousers, satisfied enough for the moment to play the cuckold and watch his wife happily take the delicious punishment she'd always craved, and he could never give.

Fil was still wanking frenetically, red-faced and groaning in pleasured agony, until distracted by the sound of two men's strangled cries.

He turned to see Flap and Dongle, released from Zag's sorcery and again themselves, but naked as newborns and still harnessed to the cart on all fours with harsh bits in their jaws. They gurgled calls for help and struggled against their bonds. Fil tried to ignore them, but gave up and hurried to unbuckle Flap first, then Dongle.

The two men had witnessed the rutting riot too, and once standing both displayed rock-hard flesh pillars of their own.

Flap's was an above average specimen for a smaller man, but its heavy-ridged, oversized purple helmet had earned him the appreciative nickname of *Ditch Digger* with the ladies of the Dog and Duck.

Dongle's turgid manhood was, unsurprisingly, of the perfect dimensions had he been an actual, if oversized, donkey. Already he was turning in circles to take in the panorama of quivering flesh, both hands throttling it like an attacking python and stroking from ball-sack to tip.

In seconds, naked females overran both men, panting and laughing their delight.

Three young barmaids with braided pigtails swarmed Flap and took him to ground, one straddling his face while the other sat his cock and the third pushed his fingers into her slit and humped.

Much to his drooling delight, Dongle watched an undraped woman of suitably bovine proportions stampede toward him, breasts, buttocks, thighs and belly oscillating like the waves of an ocean storm. He grinned stupidly and held his arms out to embrace her. Arriving, she coldcocked him with a meaty fist to the jaw, dropped him like a poleaxed steer and sat him hard, taking his donkey dick to the hilt and ululating her triumphant joy.

"Hehhuhheh!" the great dolt grunted happily, "Boom-BAM! Boom-BAM!"

On the cart, Oben and Nios had left behind all human sense. No longer two bodies of flesh and blood, she was now a rocky bay on the stormy seashore, he the crashing waves of tidal forces, pounding her with oceanic flow then ebbing to gather strength and fill again her welcoming cove. She was the whirlwind, unmercifully drawing the very air to her center; he the land surrendering every nugget of his fertile loam to her irresistible vortex.

Nios woke. Sudden and swift, profound and frightening, a door opened. They stepped through the portal. Man and woman, face to face, lay together in the molten blaze of each other's eyes. The knowledge shining in those enlightened windows turned the last silver key in the last golden lock.

Oben stopped deep inside her. She watched his face as he could only silently mouth the words, "I love you."

His dam burst. Pulsing and throbbing, he poured himself into her. Jet after jet of his hot, viscous seed flooded in and, receiving it, the sheer animal gush and the knowledge of what it engendered pushed her beyond the limits of her frailty into the realm of magic.

Both screamed in agonized exultation, their bodies undulating in unrestrained, volcanic orgasms. The waves of ecstasy crested and ebbed only to crest again, leaving them breathless until they gasped for air and repeated their song of bliss, their eyes still locked.

The wildfire magic spread and impelled every human and animal body in the arena to join in their rapture. The roars and shrieks rose and echoed from the castle walls, from the crests of the mountain, through the clouds to reach the Father and make him smile at his children's joy.

The flesh of a hundred bodies clapped thunderous applause while organs pumped hot and salty nectar into wombs, mouths, and sphincters, splashed breasts, bellies, and backs, flooded phalluses, painted pubic hair, and flecked faces. Animals brayed and howled and whinnied as humans sang along in sibling imitation.

In time, the groans and shouts of painful delight quieted into relieved laughter, sighs, and finally the wet smacking of appreciative kisses.

Oben and Nios lay quietly, letting the final throbs of their shared rhapsody slow. A deep glow of contentment spread from their conjoined flesh to limbs, hearts and minds.

They smiled and stroked cheeks and lips with gentle fingers, marveling at the simple pleasure of loving touch.

He whispered, "I am yours, and yours alone, forever, in this life and any that follows."

Her smile brightened and canted a bit, the old teasing spark returning to her eye.

She said, "I told you."

Chapter 30 - Go Big or Go Home

That night, the feast that was to celebrate a new king was instead an unusual coronation of an unusual queen.

Three long rows of tables in the great hall were full to overflowing with guests highborn and low, citizens of Tamberlain and of Aflax. They laughed, sang, and flirted together, not a sour note of animosity to assault the ear.

Men in pink and white drank to the health of those in black and red, who immediately sang praises of their Tamberlain brothers. Men and women who, in various combinations, had engaged in happy if rough rumpy pumpy at midday, now were hugging, caressing, kissing, stroking, fingering and frotting each other as they ate and drank. Others absconded into alcoves and antechambers surrounding the great hall for full-on repeats of their earlier exploits, some adding tangy man milk and lady juice to their supper fare.

Kings Otto and Hod sat at the head table, to either side of the empty seat of honor, eating and drinking ravenously, laughing at each other's jokes and lifting their cups in mutual salute.

Syllabub reigned over the festivities as a glowing, congenial hostess. She passed among the tables with a wine jug in each hand, regaling her guests with jokes and compliments, basking in their copious thanks, songs of praise to her beauty, and commendations of her impressive conjugal flexibility.

At a special table near the royals sat the new heroes Oben and Nios, Flap and Dongle, Fil and Caw.

Toasts to their health and happiness from the crowd echoed to the rafters. Oben smiled in blushing modesty while Nios beamed with delight, caroused and quaffed to honor each shouted oath.

Flap stood and bowed to each tribute, endearing him to ladies admiring his prominent codpiece and giving him a better view down the tables to sight his next amorous conquest.

Unaware of anything not set on the table before him, Dongle managed to bite, chew, drink, swallow, breathe, laugh and belch simultaneously, his bovine eyes sparkling with unadulterated, childlike glee.

Fil was giddy with drink, eating only enough to be polite to keep his hands free for goosing serving maids from across the room. His eyes gleamed with mischief as one woman after another bleated a happy gasp, feeling two fingers push knuckle deep inside her when no one was within arm's reach.

Caw had his own place setting and squawked with delight over a large silver bowl full to the brim with crawling, wriggling bugs of every type. Between pecks and swallows, he crowed and cackled to any nearby ear, reciting a long litany of the myriad wonders that flying afforded.

Servers wheeled carts among the tables to haul entire boars, lambs, beef quarters, flocks of chickens and pheasants, schools of fish and other delights from the kitchens, along with delectable greens and fruits from the royal gardens, great loaves of bread and massive, tapped hogsheads of ale.

When she finally settled, Syllabub's place at the center of the head table foreshadowed a turning point in royal history and tradition. With a king at either hand, both men obviously in thrall to her beauty, charm and durability, anyone with eyes to see would not find surprising the announcement that followed.

The queen signaled to a herald, who thumped his heavy staff of office three times on the stone floor and shouted, "My lords, ladies, gentlemen, rabble, riffraff, lechers, libertines, and all attending this royal occasion, gather near, attend and shut the fuck up! Her highness, Queen Syllabub, she of beauty fair and thighs beyond compare speaks! Ludd save the queen!"

The crowd rose and thundered, "Ludd save the queen!"

Syllabub stood, beamed a smile and said, "I thank you all for your kindness and welcome you as honored witnesses to a momentous occasion in the history of our two countries."

She offered her hands and loving smiles to Otto on her right, and Hod on her left. The men gently kissed her wrists and gazed on her with a mixture of puppy-dog devotion and rutting bull lechery seen only in those well-mated.

"As you all know, Tamberlain and Aflax have long been rivals. For generations, our kings feuded, our armies fought bloody battles, our merchants engaged in price wars and retaliatory buy-one-get-one-free First Father's Day Sales. Let us forget and forgive the origins of our animosity, and if there were insults or injuries inflicted that began the troubles, those who suffered them are long since dead and buried. It is time their children, and children's children, and children's children's children bind up the wounds that need not bleed any longer and join hands as the family we once were and can be again."

Applause and cheers rattled the enormous stones of the walls and the massive timber rafters.

"To that end, the three of us" Syllabub again gave her hands to the kings, who clasped them and rose, "have been in closed-door conference all this afternoon-"

Someone shouted, "Is that what the kids call it these days, your highness?"

"Well" said the queen, pretending to blush, "we did do a lot of talking... eventually..."

Again, the crowd laughed and cheered.

"... and from those discussions we have arrived at a royal compact, one that unites our two fair kingdoms into one."

Smiling but shocked, the crowd fell silent.

"Henceforth, the lands of Tamberlain and Aflax shall be one principality, known as Amberlax."

Someone shouted, "Ludd save Amberlax!"

The crowd again rumbled the stones with their refrain.

"We have agreed, also, that kings Otto, Hod and myself shall rule as a triumvirate, which is a fancy way of saying *threesome*... with me in the middle!"

At the queen's wink-and-nod, the guests bellowed in laughter so tinged with lewdness that several guests ran for the alcoves.

When the ruckus finally died down, Syllabub continued: "This day shall be commemorated annually as the founding day of our new nation, to be celebrated exactly as we did today, um, minus that asshole Zag..."

Sounding like a flock of geese startled into flight, ten score foreheads received protective slaps.

"... and it shall be known as the Origin Orgy of Amberlax."

A man laughed and shouted, "OOA! What I say when I come!"

There followed another round of laughter, toasts, quaffs, fondles, and through-the-trouser and under-the-skirt handjobs.

Syllabub signaled for quiet and said, "A million details wait to be discussed and decided, but for now, we wish to honor our special heroes for their loyal, brave and unbelievingly sexy service to our sovereigns and our nation!"

The queen pointed to the table where Oben and his companions sat. The guests exploded into wild celebratory shouts, cheers and choruses of the now official national grunt, *OOA!*

The six companions stood and accepted the accolades with signature aplomb:

Oben smiled and waved.

Nios raised her tankard, threw a smoky challenge of a smile and hiked her skirt to her thigh crease.

Flap bowed, then pointed to his groin.

Dongle, tankard in one hand and a half-eaten chicken in the other, shouted, "Queen good!" through a mouthful and thrust his hips.

Fil swept his hand in a broad arc and goosed every living creature in the room, down to the dogs and cats.

Caw squawked and cackled, flapping his wings and cursing Fil for the assault to his cloaca.

The queen continued, "This we will do by raising them to positions of high responsibility and authority in our new court."

The crowd hushed.

"Wizard Fil" the queen said, gesturing with an upturned palm, "we appoint you Royal Magician, Doctor and Counselor to the Triumvirate. We ask that you provide good advice, good health and the occasional magic miracle to the benefit of the sovereigns and the country. Do you accept?"

Fil pumped his fist and shouted, "You bet your sweet nipples I will, queenie!"

"Hey asshole!" cawed Caw. "What about me?"

Fil thought a moment, then bowed to the queen. "Your highness, as part of my duties, I will require a scientist of the highest caliber, and though he's a feathered, foul-tempered and foul-mouthed crow-"

"Raven, you rat fucker!"

"... Raven, Caw here is the best in all the land. If I can staff him with scribes and assistants, he will endeavor to bring the gift of flight to the people of Amberlax."

Syllabub glanced at the kings, who each nodded and saluted with their cups.

"Consider it done."

Another cheer echoed between the stone walls.

"Damn, Fil" Caw said, sniffling, "sometimes you can be a really nice asshole."

The queen gestured and said, "Archer Flap, and, uh, Squire Dongle, we appoint you Sheriff and Deputy of Fuckall, charged with securing the safety of travelers and merchants along the Forked Road, the fastest route from our castle to Barada and points east, including the unincorporated areas south-west of the mighty river Krunt. Do you accept?"

Flap bowed deeply and said, "With honor and humility, gracious queen."

Dongle chortled and jumped like a child with a new toy, then roared, "Flap good!" and backslapped his smaller friend head-over-heels to the far side of the table.

When Flap got to his feet and the laughter quieted, the queen again commanded attention.

"Our dear, beloved, and smoking hot couple, Oben and Nios. We appoint you Master and Mistress of the Horse, and charge you with the care, increase and husbandry of the royal herds, commanding all things equestrian in Amberlax. We grant you status as Royal Peers of the court, with the titles of Baron and Baroness, lands, castles and two thousand coin by the year. Do you accept?"

Nios was beside herself with joy, her face alight with shock and delight, and was about to speak when Oben said, "Well, um..."

She turned on her new husband and exchanged one face for another in a heartbeat. The face she offered Oben warned of rough weather blowing in.

"What do you mean by, 'Well, um' dear ... husband?"

His face betrayed utter surprise at her reaction.

"But darling, don't you want to go home to Barada, have our marriage made holy and legal by a priest, live simply and raise our children in a wholesome, quiet life in the village where our ancestors have thrived for a thousand years?"

The silence in the great hall was total, save for soft but enthusiastic breathing coming from a few nearby alcoves.

"Fuck, no!" she shouted.

All eyes turned to Oben.

He grinned, winked, said, "Me neither" and pinched her nipple.

She shrieked, "Ow!", grabbed her insulted breast and grinned.

Making as if to hug him, she delivered a quick slap to the underside of his testicles, buckling him to the floor.

The people gasped, smiling.

While he groaned and struggled to stand, Nios turned her bright eyes and smile on the queen and said, "We accept!"

The thunder engendered by the cheering, stomping, tankard pounding crowd shattered an ancient stained-glass window. It depicted Tayken and Nesta, their cart still full of bread and wine, surveying the Great River where they would build their castle and reign as the first king and queen of Tamberlain.

With her kings standing at her side, Syllabub shouted and whistled for quiet.

"We want to remember and honor the seventh hero of your brave troupe, who sacrificed himself to save us all. So, in his name and honor we gift to you a blessing to start your new lives as Master and Mistress of the Horse."

She gestured to the back of the hall. "Bring in Chanter's Song!"

Through the enormous doors of the hall, a page led a yearling colt with a coat as black as midnight. His long, flowing mane and tail of silken blond waved like a thousand victory pennants as he threw his head and high-stepped toward the hero's table.

Nios squealed with girlish joy and ran to caress and kiss the lively animal. He whinnied and nuzzled her neck and shoulder. Her laughter pealed like victory bells, infecting the guests with her love and happiness.

Flap smiled at the display and nudged Oben, now standing more or less upright.

"Should have named him Chanter's Cock" he said, pointing.

The colt's fully dropped sheath waved and flapped wildly as he nickered and pushed at Nios with his muzzle, frustrated that the lovely two-legged mare would not present her rump.

Everyone in the hall watched and howled with laughter, cheers and shouts of "OOA!" as Nios smiled and struggled to keep herself facing the now obviously rutting equine.

She caught her husband's eye from across the room and shouted, "What can I say? It's a gift!"

SNEAK PEEK — Sirens & Scoundrels

From the high fantasy adventure trek genre we move on to skewer a very popular type of "bodice ripper" — *The Pirate Romance.*

Sirens & Scoundrels is Tale from the Quaquaverse — my ongoing series of original novels aimed at spreading fun and laughter, thrills and chills, plus a bit of naughty pleasure thrown in just because. Each tale is unique — a new world, all new characters, themes and genres — but they all celebrate the pleasure and privilege of being human, with all the dark and light shades that color our souls.

The "Quaquaverse" is merely my fanciful dream about the source of every imaginable narrative — the metaverse of metaverses. The fountainhead of every fable, legend, myth and novel is like a blazing sun radiating stories in every direction - quaquaversally — the way a star in the cosmos radiates light. Each beam of light is a story, a world where a person lives who longs for love and adventure, a *Tale from the Quaquaverse.*

A.P. John

Sirens & Scoundrels Chapter 1 - Her Pleasure Cruise, Interrupted

Lady Ravenna Ferdinand, young and lovely and infuriatingly blond, stood on the deck watching the afternoon sun glisten on the calm waters of the Plymouth Sea as the three masted corvette *Bentley* cut deep wake under full sail to carry her homeward, there to marry and happily surrender her virginity.

"I shall miss the convent in Packard" she said wistfully, the ocean breeze hardly mussing her ludicrously long, blond, flaxen locks, "but my heart belongs to my beloved, and I am ready to give it over to him completely."

"Yes, mistress" said the short and wizened Sister Adelaide. She gripped her veil tight around her withered neck against the wind. "Two days hence you will be wed, and you have prepared yourself well."

As shining and flowing as the flag of her tresses, Ravenna's luxurious silk gown of azure blue fluttered in the wind. She pulled the delicate lace shawl tighter about her shoulders. "I'm so happy they allowed you to accompany me, dear Adelaide. Prepared or not, I feel I must have your continued guidance as I approach my wedding day and the inevitable rough-but-loving coitus that awaits me in the marriage bed."

"Well, m'lady, it need not be rough."

The rose hue in the girl's porcelain cheeks betrayed her thoughts. "No? But is it not true, as you and the sisters taught me, that a husband may take his pleasure as he will, ravishing his quarry with impassioned tongue kisses, tearing her bodice open to feast on her heaving breasts, lifting her skirts and bending her over the soft velvet bolster of the chaise lounge to-"

"Ahem" the squat nun interrupted, blushing herself, "yes, all that might indeed be your lot. But then again, the good captain might be inclined to more gentle pursuit of your tender favors."

"Might he? Oh, dear."

Ravenna turned to gaze over the prow toward the western horizon, beyond which lay the Duchy of Hudson. The fast ship would make port there in a few brief hours, returning the lady to her home after a year in convent. Her father, the Duke Argo, and her mother, the Duchess Gleda, awaited her arrival, making lavish preparations for her wedding to the brave and impeccably groomed Captain Ozymandias Wembleye.

"I do hope not," she whispered.

A deckhand hurried to the women and held out a parchment, carefully folded and sealed with a red wax stamp.

"Beggin' yer pardon m'lady, but this arrived with our cargo 'afore we left port at Packard this mornin.'"

Ravenna took the envelope and ignored the sailor as she read the salutation.

When Adelaide saw the man staring lustfully at the young lady's taut but ample breasts, she reached out and gave his ballsack a quick slap.

He grunted and doubled over, eyeing the old woman with surprise, then scorn.

"Off with you" the angry nun growled, "or take my foot to thy yarbles, thou starveling bulls-pizzle."

As the man limped away, Ravenna's eyes blazed with joy.

"It's from my beloved Oz!" she gushed, bouncing on the balls of her feet with excitement. Her thick, irritatingly shiny hair flashed semaphore in the deepening late-day sunlight.

She broke the seal and spread open the parchment, scanned the first line and announced, "I must retire to my quarters to read my dear captain's love letter properly. Are all my belongings stowed aboard this vessel?"

"Yes, dear girl, but only the trunk with your essentials has been placed in your cabin."

"Then go and fetch the Penis Portmanteau immediately and return as quickly as possible. I must prepare!"

"At once, mistress" said the aged sister.

As Adelaide shuffled off toward the cargo hold, Ravenna skipped girlishly to the small room allotted her near the captain's cabin and closed the door behind her. She twirled with delight several times, holding the letter to her breast, then stopped and closed her eyes, her breath shallow and fast.

"Oh my dear, dear Captain Ozymandias" she whispered, "how long we have been apart. But soon we will become one in wedlock and never be separated again."

Thinking back on her year of training at the hands of the Sisters of Saint Salacious, her eyes sparkled, and her grin turned wicked.

"Won't you be surprised" she purred, "when you learn how ready I am to receive your animal lust."

She opened the parchment and began reading aloud.

To My Darling, the Lady Ravenna Ferdinand, Song of My Heart.

The girl caught her breath and sighed, then read on.

This morning I enjoyed a particularly splendid bath. The water was a perfect middling temperature, not overly hot but not tepid, and the bubbles ideal in volume and texture so as to form a lovely relief map of peaks and valleys. The scented soap delivered a delicious admixture of lavender and rosemary, sweet and savory, and so naturally my thoughts drifted toward you and the nearness of our upcoming nuptials, now a scant few days off.

Transported as she read, Ravenna's delicate fingers drew a soft line from the hollow in her throat to a point deep within her cleavage. She felt herself stir, warmth infusing her inner thighs. She read on, now too breathless to speak the words, able only to mime them with pale, trembling lips.

I am told your father and mother have devoted considerable time and resources to the ceremony of our joining...

Ravenna balked and gasped slightly, her mind afire with wanton images associated with the word *joining*.

... and so we are assured a lavish affair, full of pomp and parade. If you don't deem it impertinent of me, I believe I shall array myself in my finest dress whites with the royal blue piping and gold epaulets and adorn my best fore-and-aft bicorne with the largest ostrich plume I can obtain. Would that please you, my dove?

"Yes" the lady breathed, "yes, my darling man, it would please me to clutch those epaulets while your many heavy medals swing and ring like bells as you hold me down and..."

The door suddenly opened to reveal Adelaide dragging a heavy case of leather and brass.

"Here, dear lady" she wheezed, "your selections."

Ravenna sat heavily on the small bed and fought to catch her breath. "Hurry, dear sister, bring it here!"

The aged nun huffed as she struggled to carry the heavy valise. She grunted and heaved it onto a bedside table, undid the latches and raised the lid.

Within, nestled in deep purple velvet, lay seven phalluses carved of various hard materials, each one a true portraiture of that which the Captain Ozymandias Wembleye carried within his breeches.

The first, sculpted of finely grained white oak and polished to a sheen, depicted his manhood at rest, peering down over the double-domed encasement of his testicles. The seventh bore the likeness of his fully turgid cock and balls, carved of the finest white marble and given life by the artist's anatomical details of veins on the shaft rising toward the prominently ridged glans.

The remaining artifacts depicted the captain's wedding tackle in the various stages of rest and activity between the two extremes.

It was with such a set of artisanal dildi that the good Sisters of the Saint Salacious Convent trained young brides-to-be to recognize the various stages of male priapic station, what techniques could be employed with each for both her and her husband's pleasure, and to help avoid the typical shock and awe that virginal brides had throughout history been forced to endure during the first attempt at post-ceremony penetration.

Ravenna greedily snatched the seventh from its velvety bed, hiked her skirts to her hips and, legs wide and shaking, plunged it to the hilt into her already bemoistened and quivering quim.

"Ah!" she cried. "Yes, my lusty sea dog! I am helpless against your onslaught of mean-spirited fuckery!"

While one hand impaled herself with the marble manroot, the other lifted the letter to her squinting eyes. Struggling to focus her vision, she continued to read aloud between rhythmic grunts and sighs.

When I think of you, my dear Ravenna, and of our impending union in wedded bliss, my heart soars with delight at the thought of sharing not only our conjugal bed...

Ravenna grunted and snarled, "Yes! Harder, you seagoing stallion!"

... but also our conjoined bathing facilities, where I look forward to long and indulgent sessions of lavation together. I picture myself washing and conditioning your lovely tresses...

Panting, Ravenna growled, "Fill your fist with my locks and spur me on to the finish line, master of horse!"

... and I hope you will find my wide knowledge of oils and creams, scents and conditioning rinses impressive enough to allow me to school you in the finer details of the ablutionary arts.

Head back and eye-rolling in animalistic fervor, Ravenna dropped the letter and two-handed herself into a chest-heaving, spittle-flecking frenzy, no longer possessing the skill of human language or even knowledge of herself beyond the sensations between her navel and her knees.

Watching all this from a safe distance, Adelaide noted her lady's techniques, positions and nuances, committing to memory what advice she would offer for improvement after the girl had regained her breath and sense following yet another shattering orgasm.

A deep boom from somewhere beyond the ship caught the nun's attention. While the girl desperately steam-pistoned herself, Adelaide listened to an eerie, shrieking noise growing louder and closer, diving in dissonant glissando from high pitch to low.

The crash of iron against the wood hull shook the mighty ship as if God had slapped at a toy boat in the bath.

Ravenna sat up in confusion, her forelocks plastered to her face with sweat, the phallus half submerged, and gasped, "Did I do that?"

From beyond the door, the two women heard the panicked cries of the sailors as they ran from prow to stern shouting angry orders.

"To port! To port he comes! Below and man the cannons ya dogs!"

Adelaide hurried to the door, opened it and ran out to the quarterdeck in time to see the blur of an iron ball as it splintered one of the mainsail yard arms, sending the massive spar crashing to the deck and crushing a man beneath its weight.

The first officer appeared, blood trickling from a scalp wound and his eyes wild with panic. He pushed Adelaide back into the room, muttering curses and prayers.

"Stay within!" he shouted. "he's still a way off and we may yet prevail, but you must lock yourselves away in case he boards us!"

Ravenna smoothed down her skirts and collected herself enough to ask, "In case *who* boards us?"

"None other than the rapacious bastard himself, m'lady. Noxious Knox Bloodworthe, the Scourge of the Seaways!"

"Saint Salacious, preserve us!" prayed Adelaide, hand to her heart.

"Bolt the door, ladies, and let none enter until we have achieved victory!"

With those words, the officer ran off, barking orders to his scattered crew.

Adelaide slammed shut the door, twisted the iron key in the lock and secured it in her habit pocket. She turned to her lady with wide, watery eyes of sheer terror.

Denied the satisfaction of her finish, Ravenna laid the now honey-slicked limestone lingam into its resting place, pulled her long, sweat-wetted hair away from her face and said to her matron, "The officer did say *rapacious*, did he not?"

Don't miss out!

Visit the website below and you can sign up to receive emails whenever A.P. John publishes a new book. There's no charge and no obligation.

https://books2read.com/r/B-A-IXVBB-LWNRC

BOOKS 2 READ

Connecting independent readers to independent writers.

Also by A.P. John

Tales from the Quaquaverse
A Horse for My Kingdom
Sirens & Scoundrels

Watch for more at apjohn-author.com.

About the Author

Since I was a kid, I've loved creating comic parodies of famous stories and movies, songs, TV shows and popular culture overall. My high school buddies and I competed to crack each other up with intricate satire, farce, and takeoffs of anything and everything. We created fake album covers, substituting fellow students for the artists, with sendups of the song titles, lyrics and liner notes. We wrote and recorded audio sketch comedies and created a fake religion complete with evangelical tract books and prayers.

So, I get immense pleasure from writing the *Tales from the Quaquaverse* novels. Each is an entirely new world with all new characters rendered as comic parodies of famous novel genres — High Fantasy, Pirate Romance, Space Opera, Detective Noir — with many more in the works. The common thread will be fierce and sexy female leads, comedy high and low, and steamy, explicit romance. I call them fantasy sex comedies. My old school pals would love them. Hope you do too.

Read more at apjohn-author.com.